"She doesn't remember you, Liam."

Liam let out a strangled sound that caused her to flinch.

Liam. It was a nice name. Strong. Solid. He was good-looking. Rugged. He had dark brown hair. His warm blue eyes radiated an intensity that unnerved her.

And he couldn't seem to take his eyes off her.

Liam ran a shaky hand over his face. "Wh-what are you talking about, Boone?"

The sheriff still had a hold on Liam. They were face-to-face, staring each other down. Electricity crackled in the room. What had Sheriff Prescott told Liam over the phone?

Liam shook his head in disbelief. His face held a dazed expression. He swung his gaze back toward her. "Ruby," he said, brushing off the sheriff's grip. He took two steps toward her. She held her ground without retreating. "I can't believe it's you. I feel like I'm dreaming. You're back!"

"I don't remember you. Or this town," Ruby blurted out. She tilted her chin up, locking gazes with him. "I'm sorry."

Belle Calhoune grew up in a small town in Massachusetts. Married to her college sweetheart, she is raising two lovely daughters in Connecticut. A dog lover, she has one mini poodle and a chocolate Lab. Writing for the Love Inspired line is a dream come true. Working at home in her pajamas is one of the best perks of the job. Belle enjoys summers in Cape Cod, traveling and reading.

Books by Belle Calhoune

Love Inspired

Alaskan Grooms

An Alaskan Wedding
Alaskan Reunion
A Match Made in Alaska
Reunited at Christmas

Reunited with the Sheriff
Forever Her Hero
Heart of a Soldier

Reunited at Christmas

Belle Calhoune

ISBN-13: 978-0-373-71997-6

Reunited at Christmas

This edition published by arrangement with Love Inspired Books.

www.Harlequin.com

Printed in U.S.A.

Beareth all things, believeth all things,
hopeth all things, endureth all things.

—*1 Corinthians* 13:7

For my father, Fred C. Bell, who always worked hard to make Christmas a wonderful time for his children. And for paying all of my outrageous library fines I accrued over the years.

Acknowledgments

For my family... Thanks for always listening to all my story ideas and giving me a thumbs-up.

For all the readers who have been asking for more stories set in Love, Alaska. Thank you for embracing the Alaskan Grooms series.

For my editor, Emily Rodmell,
for all of your support and enthusiasm for
Liam and Ruby's love story.

Chapter One

Dr. Liam Prescott had always loved Christmas. When it came right down to it, there was no place he would rather be celebrating the holiday than in his hometown of Love, Alaska. Candy canes. Twinkling lights. Peppermint hot chocolate at the Moose Café. Pine trees at the ready for decorating. Caroling from door to door. Normally there wasn't a single thing about it he didn't enjoy.

He'd been putting up a brave front these past few weeks, but he still felt as if he had a huge hole in the middle of his heart. It was especially hard over the holidays to deal with the loss of a loved one.

This year he would focus on Aidan. It would serve as a distraction from everything they had lost two years ago. The sound of his four-year-old son's tinkling laughter as he enjoyed the spirit of the season would be the highlight. To see it unfold through Aidan's eyes would be wonderful. Despite the fact they were still grieving, he wanted to give his son the most memorable Christmas ever. Although he would try his best to enjoy the festive season, it was still incredibly difficult. The loss of his wife in an avalanche search-and-rescue mission two years ago continued to sit heavily on his chest like an anchor.

Liam walked down Jarvis Street, pausing to peer through the window of the five-and-dime so he could check out the toys on display. So far he had a few items stashed away for Aidan, but nothing that would knock his socks off. He needed something fantastic that Aidan could rip open on Christmas morning and feel ecstatic about. Maybe if he focused on his son's joy he wouldn't have to deal with his own pain.

He regarded the red toboggan with a critical eye. Red was Aidan's favorite color. His son was getting to the age where he wanted to fly down the smaller hills in town without his father cramping his style. *I'm a big boy, Daddy.* Aidan's words buzzed in his ears. His pluck and grit made him smile.

Every day Aidan was growing, both physically and emotionally. He was starting to ask questions about his mother and the tragedy that had befallen her and irrevocably changed both their lives. Liam always tried to be as honest as possible, while still protecting his son's innocence. He wished that he could tell Aidan that he himself understood why Ruby had been taken from them. But he didn't understand. Not one little bit.

People often said losing a loved one was like navigating a treacherous, winding river. As far as he was concerned, it was much worse. He knew he should have pushed past the initial overwhelming grief stage, but every time he thought about his sweet, beautiful Ruby, he found himself floundering in a tidal wave of loss.

How did a person ever make peace with losing the love of a lifetime? He still hadn't found an answer to that question. Liam had come to terms with the idea that he had to move forward with his life, but he still ached for Ruby. He still agonized about the things he could have done differently. He continued to ask God why He hadn't spared her.

The insistent buzz of his cell phone had him digging in his coat pocket. A quick glance at the screen displayed his brother Boone's number at the sheriff's office.

He tapped the phone with his finger. "Hey, Boone," he answered as he took the call "What's going on?"

"Where have you been? I've been calling you for the last hour." Boone's voice had a frantic quality.

"I'm right here on Jarvis Street, heading back to the clinic," Liam explained. "I just finished eating a few minutes ago."

Liam had stopped in to eat lunch at his other brother's coffee bar, the Moose Café. No doubt the din inside had prevented him from hearing his phone ring.

"Can you come by the sheriff's office right away? It's important." He hadn't imagined it. Boone's voice sounded tight with strain.

"What happened? Is it Jasper?" Liam asked, inquiring about their grandfather, Mayor Jasper Prescott. His pulse began to race wildly. As patriarch of the Prescott family, Jasper was well loved. At times irascible and feisty, he could also be tender and wise. And due to his heart problems, they had almost lost him not too long ago. His health was a constant source of worry.

"No, it's not Jasper. You have to prepare yourself—" The line crackled. Boone's voice was swallowed up by static.

"Boone! Boone!" he called out. "I can't hear you. The call is breaking up."

"Urgent. Need to tell you—" A crackling sound came across the line. Suddenly the call dropped.

Something was wrong. Liam had heard it in his older brother's voice. The sheriff's office was only a few minutes away. Rather than call Boone back, Liam decided to head straight over to his office. *Please, Lord. Let my family be safe and sound. We already dealt with the worst when we lost Ruby! Don't let anything take us down that road again.*

Liam raced down the street, barely pausing to say hello to passersby as they greeted him. As a doctor here in town, he had a lot of clients who loved to stop him for a chat whenever he passed by. There was no time for that today. There had been something strained in his brother's tone that Liam had found alarming. He pushed open the door to the sheriff's office and rushed inside. Shelly, Boone's receptionist, stared at him with wide eyes. Fear skittered through him. Normally she greeted him effusively.

What in the world is going on?

Shelly pointed toward Boone's office without saying a single word. With his heart in his throat, Liam thrust the door open without even knocking. Boone was standing in front of his desk, his head bowed. There was a woman seated in the chair facing his desk. All Liam could see was the back of her head and shoulders.

"Sorry to interrupt your meeting. The call cut out, so I headed straight over here." The words tumbled from Liam's lips. His chest was rising and falling rapidly. He felt almost breathless.

Boone held up his hands. "Liam. Let's go in the next room. I need to talk to you." His face had a gray tinge. His jaw was tightly clenched.

Just as Boone stepped toward him, the woman turned her head around, allowing him to see her face head-on. It was a face that had been seared to his heart, mind and soul for eight years. Long, dark brown hair. Brown eyes flecked with caramel. Café-au-lait-colored skin. A heart-shaped face.

Liam let out a guttural cry. He felt a falling sensation, as if someone had pushed him off the highest branches of a mighty oak tree. For a moment he couldn't get a breath. There was no way he could utter a single word.

"Steady!" Boone said, grabbing hold of his arms as his knees buckled underneath him.

The room began to spin. He pressed his eyes closed. What was happening to him? Nothing was making sense at the moment. Everything in his world had turned upside down.

When he opened his eyes again, she was still sitting there, regarding him with a shuttered expression on her face. Ruby. His wife. The only woman he had ever loved.

Although she had been declared dead approximately two years ago in a failed search-and-rescue mission in Colorado, she was now sitting in Boone's mahogany chair, looking very much alive and well.

* * *

Ruby stood from her chair, wanting to be on the same level as the sheriff and the man he'd referred to as Liam. It already seemed as if she was at a distinct disadvantage in this situation. Having amnesia meant she had no tangible memories of this fishing village in Alaska, nor did she recognize the man named Liam who looked as if his legs might buckle underneath him. She was still getting used to the name Ruby. For the first year after her accident she'd called herself Kit until she had remembered her real name.

Sheriff Prescott hadn't told her who he had been on the phone with earlier, although she had heard him speak in an urgent tone. Next thing she knew, Liam had crashed into the room like a man on a mission.

All she felt at the moment was an overwhelming sense of fear. It was the same emotion she'd been battling for the last two years. Her legs were shaking like crazy. Coming to Love, Alaska, had been an act of pure bravery on her part. She had wanted to face her nebulous past so she could move forward with her life. And now, caught in this uncomfortable moment, she found herself wishing she had stayed back home in Colorado.

Home? That was a misnomer. She hadn't yet found a place to call home. Perhaps she never would. After seeing a story on the news about a matchmaking program called Operation Love, she had experienced a strong feeling of connection with the town featured in the report—Love, Alaska. As a result, she had ventured all the way there in the hope of getting answers. And standing here before her was a man who might be able to provide them for her.

Her entire body froze. There was so much emotion etched on the man named Liam's face. The way he was looking at her caused something to tighten in her chest. There had been a look of absolute shock, followed by an expression of such joy that it made her want to sob. The sheriff hadn't told her anything about who this man was, but she knew instinctively that he had been a huge part of her life. His reaction to her presence spoke volumes.

"Ruby!" Liam's voice sounded raspy and filled with surprise. He moved toward her with his arms open. She took a step backward, overwhelmed by the thought of being touched by a stranger. The sheriff held him back, and Ruby heard him say, "She doesn't remember you, Liam."

Liam let out a strangled sound that caused her to flinch. It was infused with pain.

Liam. It was a nice name. Strong. Solid. He was good-looking. Rugged. He had dark brown, chin-length hair. His warm, blue eyes radiated an intensity that unnerved her. He was tall, with a rangy build. And he couldn't seem to take his eyes off her.

She shifted from one foot to the other, feeling the heat from his intense gaze, folded her arms across her chest and watched the interaction between the two men. She was good at picking up on cues. It was a skill she had honed ever since her amnesia diagnosis. These men were close. Brothers or best friends, she imagined.

Liam ran a shaky hand over his face. "W-what are you talking about, Boone?"

The sheriff still had a hold on Liam. They were face-to-face, staring each other down. Electricity crackled in the room. What had Sheriff Prescott told Liam over the phone?

"She showed up here looking for any information we could provide about her past or family connections. From what I've been able to piece together, she sustained a head injury that led to amnesia. She was living in a remote area of Colorado until a recent move to Denver." Boone let out a sigh. "I couldn't believe it when she walked into my office."

Liam shook his head as if in disbelief. His face held a dazed expression. He swung his eyes back to her. "Ruby," he said, brushing off the sheriff's grip. He took two steps toward her. She held her ground without retreating. "I can't believe it's you. I feel like I'm dreaming. You're back!"

"I don't remember you. Or this town," Ruby blurted. She tilted her chin up, locking gazes with him. "I'm sorry," she said in a brusque voice. "But you need to know that before you get your hopes up."

His face fell. It made her want to cry to see him so torn up inside. And to know that it was due to her. But she wasn't going to mince words. Raising his hopes would be cruel.

"What do you remember?" he asked, his voice sounding ragged.

"Flashes. Moments. Bits and pieces. Something about this town feels familiar. My name," Ruby said. "Although for a long time I couldn't remember it, so I came up with another name for myself."

The sheriff moved forward. "Her doctors said it's retrograde amnesia."

"Retrograde amnesia," Liam mumbled. He appeared to be a bit dazed. "I—I don't understand."

"In my case they theorized that due to a head trauma I lost all my memories from before the accident," Ruby explained. "I get flashes from time to time, but they're disconnected and not grounded to anything solid. Sometimes it feels like a really fast slide show."

Liam met her gaze. "Will the memories eventually come back?"

Ruby shrugged. "Some people do recover their memories, but the doctors have told me there's no way of knowing whether mine will return."

"So you don't remember marrying me? Or being my wife?" Liam asked. His jaw trembled.

"A-are you really my husband?" she asked. She jutted her chin in Boone's direction. "He wouldn't tell me anything when he called you. He wouldn't even tell me who he was on the phone with. Needless to say, I don't like being kept in the dark. It's pretty much been the story of my life for the last few years."

"My name is Liam Prescott. I'm Sheriff Prescott's brother. And, yes, you're my wife," Liam said. Tears misted in his eyes. He ran his hand over his face. "I'm so sorry, Ruby, that you don't remember any of this."

Although on some level she knew there was a possibility this man was her husband, just hearing the words come out of his mouth served as a jolt.

Ruby couldn't help but let out a gasp. The news made her feel wobbly. She should have been prepared for this since the slight indentation on her ring finger had caused her to question whether she was a married woman. But where was her ring? Had she lost it during whatever traumatic incident had caused her amnesia?

And why else would the sheriff have called Liam down here? Liam's emotional reaction made perfect sense now. He was a man whose wife had been presumed dead for several years. And now she was back with no warning and nothing to prepare him for the startling sight of her.

"If you're my husband, then who is Aidan?" she whispered. It was staggering to find out that this gorgeous, emotional and rugged man belonged to her. Although she had always had a niggling sensation of having been married, there had been no flashes of this man or events from their life together.

Liam's blue eyes lit up. Relief swept across his features. "So you do remember something? You remember Aidan?"

She shook her head, her long hair swirling about her shoulders. "No, I don't. I've been wearing this. At first I thought it might be my name even though it sounded masculine." She held up the necklace that had been hidden from sight under her winter coat. The name Aidan had been etched on the gold pendant in flowery script.

Emotion flickered in his eyes. "I gave that to you as a birthday gift. You wore it every day without fail."

"What does it mean? Who is Aidan?" she asked, voicing the question she'd been asking herself for two years. The necklace had become important to her—it had been the only tangible thing tying her to the life she couldn't remember.

Liam seemed to be searching her eyes for clues. "He's our child, Ruby. Yours and mine."

Child. Hearing that single word served as a kick in the gut. She had often wondered if she was a mother. If she was being completely honest with herself, she had known deep down in her soul that she was somebody's mama. She remembered bits and pieces. Nothing more than fragments.

The smell of talcum powder. Cradling a newborn in her arms. Singing a soothing lullaby. A tuft of dark hair.

She sank back down into the chair, overwhelmed by the knowledge that Aidan was her son. "How old is he?" she asked, her voice a notch above a whisper. It felt strange asking questions about her own child. But she wanted to know. She needed answers.

"He'll be five in a few weeks," Liam said. A hint of a smile played around his lips.

"Five," she said with a nod. "That's a great age." Why had she just blurted that out? What did she know about five-year-olds?

"He's a wonderful boy. You'd be proud of him," Liam said. "You two used to be inseparable."

Ruby had no idea what to say to that. It hurt terribly to know that she couldn't remember precious moments with her own flesh and blood. A child she had carried in her womb and given birth to and nurtured. A boy who had been emotionally tied to her. Pain unlike any she'd ever felt before ricocheted through her. She had felt lost ever since she'd woken up in Colorado with no memories of who she was or where she belonged. Although she hadn't thought it possible to feel more agony, finding out about her son and husband filled her with a sense of yearning to fill all the holes in her memory.

They must have loved her, and in return, she must have loved them back.

Lord, please help me. I've been stumbling around in the dark for so long. But now a big bright light is being shined on my past and yet I feel nothing but confusion. I'm still uncertain about who I am and where I'm going. I'm a mother and a wife, but I'm not sure I know how to be either of those things.

Liam shoved his hand through his hair. He let out a huff of air and exchanged a look filled with hidden meaning with the sheriff. "Aidan. I have to bring you to see him, Ruby. He prays for you every night."

Ruby raised her hand to her trembling lips. Just thinking about a little boy uttering prayers for her was enough to make her come undone. *He's not just any little boy,* her voice buzzed in her head. *He's your son. Your flesh and blood.* That raised the stakes even higher.

She shook her head as a tidal wave of emotions rolled over her. Trudy and Ezra had been concerned about this very thing happening. They had wanted to make the trip with her, but after two years of being under their wing, she had needed to do something without their sheltering arms.

But everything was rushing at her now, like a freight train at maximum speed. Suddenly she started taking rapid breaths of air. It felt like she couldn't breathe. She folded her arms around her stomach and began deeply breathing in and out.

"Ruby! Are you all right?" Liam took the final few steps toward her, quickly swallowing up the distance between them. She felt his hands touching her. There was something comforting about his hands resting on her shoulders. It was the oddest thing, since he was technically a stranger to her, and she always felt wary of people she didn't know.

"It might be a good idea to give her some space," Boone said to Liam. "This could be very overwhelming for her," he explained, casting Ruby a concerned glance.

With a begrudging look on his face, Liam took a few steps back. Boone followed suit.

"If you're not feeling well, I can get you something to drink or take you to my clinic," Liam said. "I'm a doctor here in town."

Liam was a doctor? She shouldn't be surprised by the news. He exuded a kind and authoritative air. It wasn't hard to imagine him treating patients or calming a distraught child who needed shots. Ruby didn't know whether there was a part of her that was remembering something from the past or whether it was strictly her imagination, but a picture of Liam outfitted in a white lab coat, a stethoscope hanging around his neck, flashed before her eyes.

"I'm fine," Ruby said. "I think everything is just catching up to me." She rubbed the back of her neck. "The plane ride. Being back here. I know you're saying this is where I'm from, but I feel like a newborn filly finding its legs."

"Ruby, I know this can't be easy for you, but this is a blessing for our family. God answered our prayers." He locked eyes with her. "And now I need to bring you back home where you belong so you can reunite with Aidan."

Oh, no! She didn't think she was quite ready for

that. Ruby wanted to see her child, but she was terrified. What would she say to him? Would he expect her to be a certain way or hold him in a special manner? She didn't know a single thing about being a mother.

"I hadn't planned on anything like this," she said lamely. "I—I don't know what I would say to him. How do I explain that I don't remember him?"

"If you don't face this, you might never really be able to move forward." Liam's voice held an intensity that reverberated throughout the room. "Part of that is meeting your son."

Ruby bit her lip. A feeling of anxiety swept over her. Had coming to Love been a huge mistake? Everything was happening so quickly. In a matter of minutes her life had dramatically changed, so much so that she wasn't sure she could keep up with all the shifts.

"Can Ruby and I have a moment alone?" Liam asked, looking over at the sheriff, who nodded before stepping out of the room.

Once they were alone, Ruby felt a sudden shyness take over. This tall, good-looking man with the soulful, intense eyes was her husband. He belonged to her. And she to him. The weight of it settled over her like a warm blanket. Even though she couldn't remember him or any specific details about their life together, she felt a tremendous pull in his direction that shook her to her very core. She fought against a sudden impulse to run all the way back to Colorado where she'd been safe from this gorgeous, rugged man who seemed to want the world from her.

Chapter Two

Once they were alone, Liam took a moment to simply gaze at his wife. She was even more beautiful than before, he realized. If that was even remotely possible. Since the very first time he had laid eyes on her, he'd believed that Ruby was the loveliest woman in the world. She had the type of beauty that turned heads. Her warm brown eyes had always showed him her truths. Now, he couldn't see anything radiating from their russet depths but fear.

And it killed him that instead of making her feel safe, his presence brought her anxiety. Hadn't Ruby always sought him out for love and protection? At least she had until the last few weeks before the accident in Colorado. He'd never admitted it to a single person, but his marriage had been coming apart at the seams. They had fought over the dangers of her occupation and Liam's desire to have her close to home rather than flying out on rescue missions. Now, with Ruby's memory loss, he was still the only person who knew she had asked for a separation before heading to Colorado.

"You can trust me, Ruby. I'm not going to do anything to hurt you," he said, moving toward her slowly so as not to startle her. At the moment she resembled a deer caught in the headlights. His insides twisted painfully at the sight of her discomfort. He could only imagine how difficult it would be to come face-to-face with a past you couldn't remember.

"That's not what I'm worried about. I don't want to hurt Aidan." She twisted her fingers together and bowed her head.

His heart leaped at the sight of it. It had been a tic of Ruby's whenever she was nervous. It was reassuring to know that she had still retained something about herself that he recognized. Even though she couldn't remember him or their life together, this was still Ruby, despite the obvious changes in her demeanor. His wife. The woman he had vowed to love for a lifetime.

Something told him he might be repeating this mantra over and over again in the weeks and months to come.

"Hurt him?" Liam asked. "That's not possible. He's going to be over the moon to have his mother back."

She lifted her head up and looked at him, her expression mournful. "But I won't be the same mother who raised him. I'm a different person now, and I know that must be confusing and heartbreaking to you, but the accident changed all that."

Her words popped his euphoria like the bursting of a balloon. This wasn't nearly as straightforward as he would like to believe. The woman standing before him wasn't his Ruby.

"What happened to you?" he blurted. He had so

many questions about where Ruby had been for the last few years and how she had lived. Ever since he had walked into Boone's office they had been churning inside him like acid.

A sigh slipped past her lips. "I was in an accident, I think. I've had CT scans on my head, and it's pretty apparent that I suffered a traumatic brain injury. I don't know exactly what happened, but when I woke up I was in a remote, wooded area." She shook her head. "I must have wandered there in a daze from the mountain. God must have been watching out for me."

"You were in Colorado doing a search-and-rescue operation." He smiled at her. "That was your job. You were really great at it, too. You were caught up in an avalanche when you were doing a mountain rescue."

Ruby's jaw dropped. "Search and rescue? I had no idea. The reason I came to Love was because of a news story I watched on television about the Operation Love program. It basically detailed how the town mayor was matching single bachelors from here in town with women from all over the country." She furrowed her brow. "There was something so familiar about the town. And I couldn't get it out of my mind for days and days after I watched the segment. It gnawed at me. Call it a gut feeling, but I knew there was some connection between this quaint village and my old life. So I made the decision to fly out here and do some digging. I hit pay dirt the moment I entered your brother's office. He practically hit the floor the moment he laid eyes on me."

"Can't say I blame him," Liam murmured. "I had the same reaction."

"It's understandable. It's been two years since the accident."

"My dad was there that day in Colorado, helping out with the operation. He's search and rescue like yourself. He saw you get swallowed up by the snow-slip, along with three others who were standing on that mountain ledge." Just recalling it sent shivers through his body. It had been the darkest day of his life.

Ruby's brown eyes widened. "Did they make it?"

"No," he said somberly. "Only one body was recovered. All three of you were presumed dead."

Tears pooled in Ruby's eyes. "I have no idea how I survived that. All I know is that I was discovered by a couple who live in a remote area, miles away from the mountain. I don't have a clue as to how I got there, but my friend Trudy spotted me wandering aimlessly near their cabin. When she brought me inside she said I was disoriented and couldn't even remember my name. For the first few months she and her husband called me Kit. Then I remembered my name. It just came to me out of the blue."

Liam felt a burst of anger toward the couple who had taken Ruby in. He clenched his teeth and reminded himself to count to ten so he didn't vent. "How in the world didn't they connect you to the rescue operation on the mountain? It was in all the papers and on the internet."

Ruby quirked her mouth. "The couple who rescued me lives off the grid. Their lifestyle is very humble. They don't have television or internet. And they were very protective of me. They brought in a doctor who examined me at their home since I was too afraid to leave. There was a bump on the back of my head, along with bruised ribs and some contusions. He wanted me to come in for additional testing, but I refused any further medical intervention."

"You're incredibly fortunate there wasn't bleeding on the brain or anything else that might have been fatal." Liam hated sounding like a medical know-it-all, but he couldn't help but see this from a doctor's vantage point. Not seeking medical attention at a hospital had been foolish. And risky.

Ruby sent him a sheepish look. "Not too smart of me, I know. I was a wreck for months and months. I jumped at the slightest sound, and I refused to do anything outside of my narrow comfort zone. It wasn't until I went to Denver that I began to get connected with modern-day living. That's when I finally had medical tests to get a firm diagnosis."

"I'm amazed that you went so long without medical attention," Liam said with a shake of his head. "But I understand that your circumstances were extreme. Having no memories must have been terrifying."

"It was," Ruby said with a sigh. "I don't want to say I'm used to it now, but nothing is as bad as those first few days and weeks when nothing made sense. Lately I've experienced more flashes of memory. I'm grateful that I remembered my name and this town…even though I have to admit it's not easy being here."

Liam observed the worry lines and strain etched on her face. He wanted to reach out and take away all her fears and worries. Back when things were good between them he would have reached out and swept a kiss across her brow and soothed Ruby the way he knew best. If only he could. Those days felt like a million years ago.

He smiled at her. "I feel very grateful that those flashes led you back home."

"Home." She wrinkled her nose as she said the word. "I don't want to hurt your feelings, because you seem like a very nice man, but home isn't something I've ever known. Not really. The home we shared… I wish that I could remember it, but I can't."

Liam's heart lurched at the look of utter defeat etched on Ruby's face. The woman he knew was a fighter. She had never given up on anything. Not a single time. Not ever.

"I know everything is coming at you fast and furiously. But I need you to know that when I married you I took our wedding vows very seriously…we both did. We're still married, Ruby. My home is your home."

"Liam," she protested, "what you're saying is very sweet, but I don't—"

"I know you don't remember us and our life together, but I remember you," Liam interrupted. "The food you like. What makes you laugh. Your favorite color. The way your cheeks flush when you get angry."

A vein began thrumming above her eye. "Those things may have changed. I've done a lot of research on my condition. Tastes can become altered after a brain injury. For instance, I love apples. I may not have before."

Liam grinned. It made him happy to know that she hadn't changed completely, despite the differences he noticed in her demeanor and personality. "You've always loved apples," he said. "Ever since I've known you."

"That's good to know," she said. A hint of a smile played around her lips. For a moment she looked less somber. Almost lighthearted. Within seconds, a shadow crossed her face. "I'm not sure about meeting Aidan. I don't know how to act, what to say to him."

Liam had to stop himself from reaching out and caressing her cheek. She looked so vulnerable right now. "You're his mother, Ruby. For him, that's going to trump everything else. Remember, he's only four years old. He's at the age where he accepts things at face value for the most part. Unless, of course, you're trying to get him to eat his vegetables." Liam let out a chuckle. "Aidan and broccoli have been having a tough time of it lately."

Ruby scrunched up her face. "Broccoli? Yuck. The kid has good taste. I like him already." She let out a sweet laugh.

"And I'm not an expert on amnesia, but as a physician, I know that certain things can trigger memories. Maybe seeing Aidan will cause you to remember something solid about your life before the head trauma," he said. "Something that can ground you in the here and now."

She chewed her lip for a moment. It seemed as if she was soaking in everything he had explained to her. "You're right," she said with a nod. "I owe him a shot at remembering. He's mine, whether I remember him or not. I'm not sure if I know how to be his mother, Liam, but I know it's not right to walk away from this. At least not without seeing him first."

"I'm not asking for the moon, Ruby. I just want you to meet him, to see him face-to-face. We'll cross the bridges as they come."

"I'll do it," Ruby said with an emphatic nod of her head. "I want to see our son."

Liam felt a tightening sensation in his chest. Aidan was going to be reunited with his mother! It was almost as wonderful as the moment the knowledge had seeped in that Ruby was alive. For the last two years he had been walking around like a man with half a heart. Now, for the first time in forever, he felt as if he had hope. Although he knew the odds might be stacked against Ruby getting her memory back, he couldn't help but feel optimistic about their lives returning to normal. And, above all else, Aidan getting his mother back.

With Ruby back in their world, God had just presented him and his son with the best Christmas gift ever.

Ruby sat in the passenger seat of the big, midnight-blue truck and gazed in wonder at her surroundings. She almost felt like a little kid as she swung her eyes in every direction. Everything in this village was so beautiful. It resembled an old-fashioned postcard. Jarvis Street—the main area in town—had quaint shops lit up with sparkly Christmas lights and charming lampposts decorated in red and white.

A huge pine tree sat on the town green, adorned with colored lights and an abundance of ornaments. Couples were walking hand in hand down the street while a group of children had their noses pressed against one of the shop windows. A big sign with the words Operation Love hung on a shop door. Her attention was drawn to an establishment called the Moose Café. It looked festive and fun, judging by the moose logo above the door and the customers who sailed out the door with contented smiles on their faces.

"That's my brother Cameron's place." Liam glanced over at her, as if waiting for her to react to the name he'd tossed out. It hadn't registered at all. She felt a little dip in her stomach. It felt as if she might be disappointing him by not remembering names and places and this glorious town. But she could never pretend about her memories just to make someone happy—they were sacred.

"It started as a coffee bar, but it's morphed into a pretty good restaurant," Liam explained. "He serves up a mighty good mochaccino and a whole assortment of other fancy coffee drinks."

"It seems like a great place," she said, admiring the soft glow emanating from inside. It looked like the sort of establishment where friends gathered to share food, good conversation and fellowship. Who had her friends been in this small fishing village? Had they mourned her passing? Had they missed her?

"He built that place out of sheer grit and determination. You used to always say that Cameron could do anything he set his mind to." A ring of satisfaction laced his tone.

"I guess I was right," she murmured. "That's quite commendable of him. How many siblings do you have?"

"Three. There's Boone, who you just met. He's the oldest. Cameron, who owns the Moose Café. And last but not least, is my sister, Honor. She's the baby of the family." He quirked his mouth. "I don't want to make you feel any pressure, but my little sister always thought you hung the moon. She's at the house now, watching Aidan, so she's going to be very emotional about your return. I sent Boone ahead of us so he could tell her. Be prepared for a few waterworks. That one wears her heart on her sleeve."

Ruby was thankful for the heads-up. There was nothing worse than being blindsided. She wondered if that's how Liam felt about her showing up in Love without even the slightest warning.

He must be a strong person, she realized. Liam seemed to be handling the news incredibly well, much better than she was. Her own emotions were all over the place. She could feel something bubbling up inside her and threatening to overflow. She had been so used to stuffing her feelings down in an effort to minimize the pain of not knowing her identity. It was as if someone had pulled back her layers and exposed her core. All her nerve endings were tingling.

She bit her lip. Ruby turned toward him, admiring how good-looking he was in profile. "What about me? Do I have any brothers or sisters? And what about my parents? Shouldn't you call them?"

Liam's hands tightened on the steering wheel. "Your parents are both gone, Ruby. But you do have a brother, Kyle. You raised him after your parents died in a car accident. He lives in Alaska, but not here in Love. He's a volunteer fireman. I'll call him once we get home and see Aidan."

"Were we close?" she asked. Her pulse began to race at the idea that she had a blood relative she had loved dearly enough to raise on her own.

Liam turned to her, a sheen of moisture in his eyes. "Very close. He was inspired to become a fireman after watching the work you did with search-and-rescue operations."

Ruby felt a big smile take over her face. "That's nice. It makes me feel good to know that I worked in a meaningful profession and that I impacted people's lives."

"You saved a lot of lives, Ruby. Even on that terrible day on the mountain, you rescued people. Pretty amazing, isn't it?" Liam's voice radiated a deep respect. "You were a hero."

It was fairly wonderful, Ruby thought. A feeling of pride rose inside her. There wasn't much in her day-to-day life to feel accomplished about. Back in Denver she worked at a restaurant as a waitress. It was a low-paying, boring position that left her feeling as if there had to be more to life than her current situation reflected. But with no past, no degrees to put on a résumé and no known skills, making a living had been difficult. Her boss paid her under the table and hadn't pressed her for a social security number after she'd explained her circumstances. She was thankful she was able to live a modest life on her salary, but the work didn't fulfill her in any way.

As Moose Crossing signs appeared on the road ahead and a magnificent mountain loomed in the distance, majestic and proud, the enormity of the situation crashed over her in unrelenting waves. She had stepped out on a leap of faith by making the trip to this lovely Alaskan hamlet. Leaving Colorado had pulled her out of the comfort zone she had established for herself in Denver.

Despite her fears, Ruby couldn't remember ever having felt this wonderfully alive and present.

With every passing moment she was realizing that her being here in Love came with a host of complications. She had only brought a few days' worth of clothes with her. Somehow in her mind she had imagined coming to Alaska and doing a little bit of digging around, then heading back to Colorado to continue with her life. Closure had been her objective. Finding out about her son and Liam had added a huge wrinkle to her plan. She had meaningful ties in this town. And there was nothing about Liam Prescott that made her believe he would sign divorce papers and send her on her merry way.

Truthfully, she wasn't certain that she was fully prepared to greet her old life head-on. A husband and a child? A brother? Family and friends? She wasn't sure she could handle all of these new connections without coming apart at the seams.

Liam shot a quick glance her direction. He reached out and touched her hand. She jerked it away, feeling uncomfortable at the tender gesture. Despite the circumstances, it was too intimate. She didn't know him like that.

"I'm sorry. I didn't mean to startle you," Liam said. "You looked so nervous I just wanted to reassure you. Everything will be fine."

Ruby turned her head away and glanced out the passenger-side window. *Everything will be fine.* She wasn't sure she truly believed that. Liam couldn't possibly understand her journey as an amnesia victim. He didn't know the twisted road she walked each and every day. The fear. The anxiety and stress. The frustration over not being able to access her own memories from her mind. And now she was going to have to face her four-year-old son and deal with questions she wasn't sure she was prepared to answer.

Look up, she reminded herself. It served to remind her that when things in life became jumbled or stressful, to look for God. He was always there for her. Ever present. Always faithful. Ruby didn't know where her faith had come from, but she was grateful for it at moments like this when her fear felt like a living, breathing thing that might consume her.

"We're here," Liam announced as he turned off the road and down a private, tree-lined driveway. Ruby peered out the window. Her surroundings resembled a winter wonderland. Spruce trees were everywhere. She recognized them from Colorado. They were beautiful, with full branches covered in a blanket of white.

The tires crunched noisily on the ice and snow in the driveway.

Fear skittered through her. *What have I gotten myself into by agreeing to come here*? She took a deep, fortifying breath to calm her nerves.

Liam had been right about her meeting with Aidan. What he was asking of her wasn't a lot, considering he'd been doing it alone for two years and raising their son by himself. Something was pushing and prodding at her. A feeling deep down inside her that she'd been stuffing away for months. She ached to hold her child in her arms, to give him back the mother he'd lost. It felt instinctual, but it was terrifying to imagine how she might feel if he rejected her. What if after all this time she wasn't enough?

All of a sudden everything buzzing in her head hushed and stilled as Liam's house came into view. It resembled something out of a fairy tale. Nestled in the woods and surrounded by snowcapped trees sat a small log cabin that brought to mind a rustic lifestyle. A fat, plastic snowman gave the front porch a festive air. A green pine wreath with red ribbons adorned the front door. A smattering of icicles hung from the eaves.

A sigh slipped past her lips. It was a delightful house. Perfect for raising a family and happily-ever-afters.

Had she been happy in this cozy, eye-catching home? Had all her dreams come true when she had married Liam and given birth to their baby boy? From all appearances, Ruby Prescott had been living the dream.

"We built this house from the ground up. It was your dream, Ruby, ever since you were a little girl, to live in a log-cabin home in the woods," Liam said, his eyes moistening.

"Thank you," she blurted.

Liam frowned. "For what?"

"For giving me that…the home I always wanted. It must have meant the world to me," she said, feeling a pang in the region of her heart. To have been so loved by her husband that he had made it a priority for her to have her log cabin in the woods was a wonderful thing. It spoke of devotion.

Had our life together really been so idyllic?

She felt a wave of sadness pass over her. To have lost so much—a loving husband, a dear son and a wonderful home built straight from her imagination was painful. And although Liam's home was unbelievable, she still didn't feel any sort of connection to it. Nothing had been stoked inside her except sheer admiration.

"You don't need to thank me, Ruby. Anything I ever did was based on love. And you returned those blessings wholeheartedly and without reservation." They locked gazes for a moment. Something simmered in the air between them that caused her to turn her eyes away. It was hard to wrap her head around discussing love with someone she had just met.

Liam turned off the engine and made his way to her side of the truck before she knew what was happening. He opened the door and reached for her hand, reminding her to watch her footing on the slippery ground. Knowing her boots had already caused her to slide several times that morning, she clutched Liam's elbow as she felt her foot slipping. Liam didn't flinch as her full weight leaned on him. "Sorry," she said in a low voice. "You would think I'm used to this because of all the snow we get in Colorado."

"No worries. I've got you," he drawled, causing tiny butterflies to do somersaults in her tummy. He led her the rest of the way to the porch steps, easing his stride so as not to rush her. The gesture spoke volumes to Ruby about Liam. Considerate. Caring. A true gentleman. She felt as if she was slowly but surely piecing together the clues as to what kind of man Liam Prescott was. So far he seemed like an incredible human being. She could very well imagine women tripping all over themselves to be with a guy like Dr. Liam Prescott.

Before they had even reached the top step, the front door sprung open. A young woman with long, chestnut-colored hair and gentle features stood there, her gray-blue eyes awash with tears. She looked Ruby up and down, her expression incredulous.

"Honor," Liam said in a warning voice. "Take it easy. We don't want to overwhelm her. She's just getting her bearings."

Before Ruby knew it, she found herself enveloped in an enthusiastic bear hug, the likes of which she had never before experienced. At least not that she could recall. Honor's arms were squeezing her so tightly that for a moment it felt overwhelming. She watched as Liam untangled his sister's arms from around her and gently pushed her away.

"I'm sorry. Boone said to go easy, but I couldn't help myself." She sniffed back tears, her stare never wavering from Ruby. "I'm so happy!"

Ruby sent Honor the warmest smile she could muster. This young woman seemed so sincere and good-hearted. It made her feel all warm and fuzzy inside to know that she had fostered a tight relationship with her sister-in-law. She could feel the love radiating from Honor.

Once Liam ushered her inside the house, Ruby stood in the foyer and looked around at her surroundings. The décor was warm and cozy. Cream-colored walls provided a soothing vibe while family photos on the front table provided a personal touch. She spotted a picture of herself and Liam. It was an odd sensation to see a photo she didn't remember posing for. She was gazing up at Liam adoringly. He was holding a baby boy in his arms. Most likely it was their son.

"I just can't believe it! Ruby's back. You have your family back, Liam. All of our prayers have been answered." Honor gushed as she threw herself against Liam's chest. As Ruby stood and regarded the heartwarming scene unfolding before her, she couldn't help but fret over the very real possibility of letting everyone down. Especially Aidan. She had traveled to Love to get answers her own mind couldn't provide. She hadn't even been certain that she'd been on the right path. The thought of staying there in town hadn't ever crossed her mind.

Dear Lord. Please provide some clarity. I need You now more than I ever have before. How do I embrace these people who care about me without raising false hopes about my return? My name may be Ruby Prescott, but I don't remember who that is or how to be her.

Chapter Three

Liam felt Ruby's eyes on him as he cradled Honor against his chest. He felt a spurt of sympathy for her. She looked a tad overwhelmed. There was a tight look to her expression, as if one little thing might cause her to shatter into pieces. Although he loved his baby sister to no end, she veered toward the dramatic. Ever since she was a little girl, she'd shouted her feelings from rooftops. As her big brother, Liam had always wished he could protect her from the slings and arrows of life, but he had learned through trial and error that it just wasn't possible.

He felt relieved about his decision to have Boone break the news to Honor about Ruby. There was no way he had wanted to have that conversation over the phone with his baby sister, nor had he thought it wise to simply show up with Ruby in tow. It would have been too much of a shock for Honor. As it was, she had practically strangled Ruby with her enthusiastic embrace.

Ruby hadn't seemed to remember his sister at all.

There hadn't even been a glimmer of recognition on her face.

Retrograde amnesia? Liam had heard the term, but had never dealt with a patient who suffered from the condition. As far as he knew, it was incredibly rare, which made the situation even more baffling. And he felt a little guilty about the fact that her memory loss prevented her from remembering the pitiful state of their marriage prior to the accident.

Was it right to allow her to believe things had been wonderful between them? He himself wasn't under any illusions about that, but he owed it to Aidan to try to patch their family up. There was nothing Aidan wanted more than a family of his own.

Earlier, Boone had promised that he would keep Aidan occupied until Liam could speak to him in private about his mother's return. A quick glance around confirmed that his son was nowhere in sight.

Honor moved out of his arms and wearily ran a hand across her eyes. She appeared emotionally drained.

"Where's Aidan?" he asked, knowing he had to get down to the business of talking to his son.

"Boone is keeping him occupied in his room," Honor said. "He was super excited that Uncle Boone showed up out of the blue. I bet they're playing cops and robbers."

"I better go talk to him," Liam said, addressing Ruby. "Boone can only keep him in there for so long."

"Do you know what you're going to say?" Ruby asked in a tentative voice.

Liam shrugged. "Honestly, I'm going to wing it a little bit. There's really no script to follow here. I'll be sensitive and caring, and try to help him understand it as much as any kid his age possibly could."

Ruby bit her lip. "Could you make sure to tell him that I didn't stay away by choice…that I was sick and couldn't find my way back home."

"Of course I will," he said, emotion clogging his voice, turning it raspy. Just the thought that Ruby had been out there this whole time and living in Colorado unbeknownst to him, frustrated him to no end. But he was going to focus on what today had brought him and his family. Psalm 30:5 rolled through his mind like thunder. "Weeping may endure for a night, but joy cometh in the morning."

Ruby's return had brought him immense joy. Mixed with that joy was trepidation. The road ahead wasn't going to be easy. He knew it with deep certainty.

Liam turned and walked down the hall to Aidan's bedroom. He paused for a moment to collect his thoughts, then turned the knob and stood in the doorway. Aidan and Boone were both stretched out on the floor playing checkers. It was Aidan's favorite game. He watched the two of them, a feeling of deep love welling up inside him at the sight of his big brother bonding with his son. After the sorrow that had invaded their lives over the past few years, he felt so very blessed at this moment.

He stepped into the room, causing Aidan to look up from his game. His brown eyes lit with happiness at the sight of him.

"Daddy! I've been waiting for you to come home."

"What have you been up to, A-man?" Liam bent and tousled his son's dark curls.

"I been playing with Uncle Boone." Aidan grinned.

"Running circles around me is more like it," Boone muttered.

Aidan giggled and covered his mouth.

"Hey, little man. I need to have a big-boy talk with you about something," Liam said, trying to keep his voice casual.

Aidan's eyes bulged. "Uh-oh. Did Auntie Honor tell you about the snowball?"

Snowball? "No," Liam said with a raised eyebrow. "Is there something you need to tell me?"

Aidan gulped. "You go first."

Boone and Liam exchanged a glance. Neither of them could resist grinning at Aidan's comment. For a four-year-old, he was pretty fast on his feet.

Boone sprung up from the floor and said, "I'll give you guys some time alone."

As he walked toward the door, Boone reached out and squeezed Liam's shoulder. "Let me know if you need anything," he said with a nod.

As always, his brother was proving he was a strong support system to lean on during tough times. Once Boone had closed the door behind him, Liam went and sat on Aidan's bed. He patted the spot beside him and said, "Come on over and sit down, A-man. We need to talk something out."

Aidan joined him on the bed and peered up at him, a curious expression etched on his face. "What is it, Daddy? Did I do something wrong?"

"Absolutely not," Liam said, reaching out and tweaking his nose. "You're the bee's knees as far as I'm concerned. You're the best son on the planet."

"The planet? Whoa!" Aidan said in a raised voice. "That's cool."

"You're my best buddy. We've been through a lot since we lost your mother."

Aidan made a sad face. He let out a little sigh and bowed his head.

"I know it's been hard not having a mom." Liam placed his arm around Aidan's shoulder and squeezed.

"I wish I could remember her more," Aidan said in a soft voice. "I like looking at her face in the album. It helps me make a picture of her in my mind."

Aidan's words went straight to his heart, as they always did whenever he talked about his mother. How would he ever find the right words to tell him she was alive? How could a little boy even begin to process the information?

"Aidan. Something has happened. It changes everything for us." Aidan looked up at him with wide eyes. "It's something good. Spectacular, really."

Aidan rubbed his hands together. "Oh, I love great surprises."

"Do you remember what I told you happened to Mommy? On the mountain?"

"Yes," Aidan said in a solemn voice. "She was being a hero and snow came and swallowed her up."

"Pretty much," Liam said, biting back a smirk. "Sometimes things aren't what they seem. We thought Mommy died on that mountain, A-man. But I found out today that she didn't."

"She didn't?" Aidan asked, his mouth hanging open in shock.

"No, she didn't," he answered, blinking away the tears blurring his vision. "She hit her head and she was really sick for a long time. And she's here, right out there in the living room."

"No way!" Aidan said, jumping up from the bed. "Can I see her? Can I? Can I?"

Liam couldn't help but grin at Aidan's unbridled enthusiasm. Even though things were far from perfect with regard to Ruby's return, his son's innocent take on the situation made him feel on top of the world. He had received the news just as Liam had prayed he would…joyfully.

"There's something else I have to tell you before you see her… When she hit her head, she lost her memory. So, she's still the same mommy, but she's going to have to get to know us all over again," Liam explained.

Aidan's face fell. He stuck his lip out. Tears welled in his eyes.

"Hey, buddy. What's wrong? Just smiles today. No tears, okay?"

"I just feel sad that she lost her memories," Aidan said. "That means she doesn't remember the day I was born or getting married to you. And she won't know my favorite color or the foods I like to eat." He bowed his head and focused on the carpet.

Liam reached out and lifted Aidan's chin. "But here's the thing. Since you're getting to be such a big boy, I have a huge job for you. I'm counting on you to tell your mother all about the things that matter most to you. The name of your turtle. Your favorite toy. How you like reindeer pizza better than anything else in this world." He held out his hand. "If you're up to the mission, let's shake on it."

Aidan shook his father's hand. "I can do it. I'm going to be five soon. That means I'm getting so big."

His chest was almost about to explode with love for this boy. There were certain moments he wished he could just capture in a bottle for all time. This was one of them.

It was time to make new memories. With Ruby. "How about we go out there and get you reacquainted with your mom?"

Aidan nodded his head enthusiastically. Before Liam could stop him, he raced toward the door and pulled it open. His son tended to lead with his heart in all things. A part of him wanted to wrap Aidan up in his arms to protect him from the inevitable hurts life would bring him.

Liam took a deep breath. He knew instinctively that the road ahead was going to be difficult. God had blessed his family today with the return of Ruby. But there were still so many unanswered questions, so many potential roadblocks in the future. This wasn't going to be a cakewalk by any means. He bent his head and prayed.

Dear Lord. Sustain me with Your wisdom and guidance. Help me put my family back together. Please allow Aidan to get the Christmas gift he wants most—a mother.

Ruby sat in the brightly lit, all-white kitchen with Boone, his wife, Grace and Honor while Liam was having his private talk with Aidan. Grace had just showed up at the house a few minutes ago. With her jet-black hair and blue eyes, she was stunning. Her petite frame couldn't hide the fact that she was heavily pregnant. Ruby imagined she was set to deliver any day now.

The moment she introduced herself to Ruby, Grace had put her at ease by saying, "This is the first time we've met, so no worries about not remembering me."

Ruby had heaved a giant sigh of relief. It was one less person she had to worry about feeling awkward around.

Everything in the room was pleasing to the eye, from the granite countertops to the copper pans hanging from the rack. She couldn't help herself from gazing around with a deep appreciation for the setup. Ruby nearly fell off her chair when Honor told her she had been the one to lay out the plans for the kitchen design. Everything had been done to her specifications. Dream house. Dream kitchen. From everything she had seen, her life had been fairly wonderful. She hoped the old Ruby had been thankful for her blessings.

At the moment she was about as nervous as she'd ever been, even counting earlier this afternoon when she had walked into the sheriff's office. This was all starting to feel surreal. A husband. A kid. A town full of people who knew her.

What did she know about being somebody's wife or mother? What could she possibly achieve in this situation? Having no memories of the past was a severe limitation. It didn't allow her to have any sort of frame of reference with them. The harsh reality was that they were all strangers to her. And she was sitting here among them not knowing what to say to fill the silence.

"Would you like some more tea?" Honor asked. They were sitting at the kitchen table, sipping tea, eating chocolate-chip cookies and making polite conversation. Both Boone and Honor seemed to be avoiding any topics that might get sticky. Neither one mentioned her amnesia.

"No, thanks. This green tea is delicious, though," she said, raising the cup to her lips for another sip.

"It was always your favorite," Honor said. She placed her hand over her mouth. "Oops. I hope it was okay to say that."

Ruby reached out and squeezed Honor's hand. Her wanting to touch her sister-in-law surprised her. She wasn't really comfortable having physical contact with strangers. There was something so sweet and genuine about Liam's sister. She radiated goodness, which put her at ease.

"You don't have to walk on eggshells with me, Honor. This is a very unusual set of circumstances we find ourselves in. If you have any questions, feel free to ask me. I'll try to be as forthright as I can."

Boone let out a groan. He shook his head. "You have no idea what you just got yourself into."

Honor playfully swatted him with her hand. She turned back toward Ruby. "Do you remember anything? Smells? Sights? Liam's voice?"

She thought for a moment before answering. "Yes. I do. Fragments, I call them. I remember cradling a baby. And that feeling of loving him with all my heart. But I suppose I never connected that baby to myself because I had no memory of giving birth. And I'm very eager to go to the Moose Café, because the smell of coffee always reminds me of snow." She let out a giggle. "I have no idea why, but the brain is a funny thing."

"Hello."

Ruby heard the voice before she laid eyes on Aidan himself. He was standing in the doorway of the kitchen, all sweet brown eyes and chubby cheeks. His dark curls framed a handsome little face that closely resembled his father. Something twisted inside her chest.

Ruby stood from her chair and walked toward her son. Her palms were slick with moisture. Her tongue was all twisted up and useless. For the life of her she couldn't think of what to say at this monumental moment.

By this time Liam was standing in the doorway, quietly observing the reunion.

"Hi, Aidan. How are you doing?" She pushed the words out of her mouth.

Aidan seemed to be studying her. His face was scrunched up. He was deep in thought. "You're pretty. Daddy always said you were the prettiest girl he'd ever seen," he said. "And you look just like the pictures we have."

"Why, thank you. You're just about the cutest boy I've ever seen." Ruby wasn't exaggerating due to the fact that he was her child. With his jet-black lashes and striking features, Aidan was sure to stand out in any crowd.

"That's what Auntie Honor says," Aidan cried, seeming thrilled at the compliment.

"Do you have anything you'd like to ask me?" Ruby asked, wanting to make sure he was comfortable.

Aidan nodded slowly. "Yes. I do."

"Go for it," Ruby said.

"When the snow swallowed you up on the mountain, did it hurt?" Aidan looked at her with an awed expression.

Ruby could feel the corners of her mouth twitching with merriment. Aidan's expression was so earnest. She didn't want to hurt his feelings by laughing at his question.

"Just a teensy bit," she said, holding up her thumb and forefinger to demonstrate. "But I tried to be very brave."

Aidan cast a quick glance at Liam. "Daddy always tells me that you're a hero."

She felt her chest tightly constrict as if someone was inside squeezing her heart. This little boy was sweet and endearing and wonderful. "I…I don't know," she said in a halting voice. "I wish I could remember that, but I don't."

Suddenly a crashing sound rang out in the house. Footsteps echoed on the hardwood floors.

"Liam! Where are you?" a deep voice boomed. "I need to speak with you."

Liam let out a groan and moved further into the kitchen. "Oh, no! Who told him?" he asked with a frown, his gaze shifting between Boone and Honor.

Boone held up his hands. "Don't ask me. I haven't even had time to tell Gracie yet, never mind blabbing to Jasper."

"I haven't spoken to Jasper in days," Honor said with a fierce nod. "It wasn't me."

"Who's Jasper?" Ruby asked, wondering why everyone was acting so strangely.

A man with silver-white hair and whiskers strode into the kitchen, his face appearing more animated than a cartoon character's. "Liam! I'm glad that I caught up with you. I heard the strangest rumor a little while ago that I'm determined to clear up." He shook his fist in the air. "And whoever spread this vicious rumor better run for cover. By the time I get through with them, they're going to wish they'd never let the name Prescott come out of their mouth."

"Settle down, Jasper," Liam instructed. "You know you're not supposed to let your blood pressure skyrocket."

Jasper! Mayor Jasper Prescott. She recognized the name from some searches she had done on the internet about Love, Alaska. He was the town mayor and the creator of the Operation Love campaign, the program that brought single ladies to town to match them up with single bachelors. It seemed this town had a female shortage. And women from all over the United States were flocking to this fishing village to find themselves an Alaskan groom.

If she wasn't mistaken, Jasper was Liam's grandfather.

"Liam's right," Boone said with a frown. "Calm down before you blow a gasket."

"I will do no such thing," Jasper roared. "If you knew the heinousness of this particular rumor, you'd want to run this person out of town on a rail." Jasper wiggled his eyebrows at Liam.

"Jasper, I need to tell you something," Liam said.

Before Liam could get a word out, Jasper swiveled his eyes in her direction.

He let out a guttural cry then raised his hand over his heart. "I'm seeing things. I must be having a stroke. Call a doctor."

"I am a doctor," Liam drawled. "And you're not having a stroke."

"Grandpa, it's okay," Honor said, tugging on Jasper's arm. "She's real. It's not a vicious rumor."

Jasper pressed his eyes closed and began taking deep breaths. When he opened them, he glared at his family members. "What are you trying to do to me? Send me to my grave well before my time?"

Boone snapped his fingers. "Bravo. You've stumbled upon our diabolical plan."

Jasper rolled his eyes at Boone then took a halting step in Ruby's direction. He stuck out a finger and poked her. Ruby let out a little squeak. "You are real. Ruby! Oh, Ruby. You're back. I could almost sob with happiness."

Liam tugged at his arm. "There's something you need to know about Ruby."

"She's got a problem with her brain," Aidan explained in a chirpy voice. "It won't let her memorize stuff."

"Huh? What in the world are you going on about? That's the craziest thing I've ever heard," Jasper grumbled. He stared at Ruby with wide eyes.

"It's completely true, though," Ruby said. She stuck

out her hand. "Jasper, I presume. I'm Ruby. I wish that I could say I remember you, but I don't. And you seem very memorable, by the way."

Jasper stared at her hand for a moment, his expression shuttered. Laser-sharp blue eyes roamed all over her face before settling on her eyes. "Since you don't remember me, let's get one thing straight. I don't do handshakes with pretty girls." He winked at her. "The first hug is free of charge."

For the second time in the span of an hour, Ruby found herself being enveloped in the world's tightest hug. Jasper smelled like nutmeg and coffee beans. His embrace made her feel as if she was greeting an old friend. His sincerity was palpable. Strangely enough, she didn't want the embrace to end. It felt like a safe harbor.

When they broke apart, she noticed tears sliding down his face. He wiped them away with his palm. "Whether you remember me or not, I'm feeling mighty blessed to welcome you back into the fold," Jasper said, reaching out and grasping her hand. "We've missed you."

Ruby wasn't sure how to describe what she was feeling. She felt all tingly inside, and her chest tightened with a groundswell of emotion. Although there was a wealth of information that eluded her about her life in Love, Alaska, she knew for certain that Ruby Prescott had been well loved.

"Why don't we put the kettle back on and have some hot cocoa?" Honor suggested.

Aidan clapped his hands enthusiastically. Auntie

Honor knew the exact thing to say to get her nephew's attention.

As everyone settled around the kitchen table, Liam gently pulled Ruby aside. He shook his head as a feeling of mortification slid through him. "Sorry about Jasper's over-the-top behavior. He takes some getting used to. Sort of like sushi. He's an acquired taste."

"Not from where I'm standing." Ruby smiled. "I think he's pretty amazing from what I've seen so far. He exudes such a positive vibe. And he seems to be a true original. I like that. And I get the feeling one always knows where things stand with Jasper. He doesn't seem the type to mince words."

Liam ducked his head and laughed.

"What's so funny?" she asked.

"You always were partial to Jasper. He was like the grandfather you never had. Or so you said," Liam answered. "You always took his side against me."

"Sorry about that," Ruby said in a light voice.

"It's okay," Liam conceded. "Watching the two of you getting along like a house on fire was always enjoyable."

Ruby shrugged. "I don't want to sound like a broken record, but I don't remember that...or Jasper. Although—" Ruby frowned.

"What is it?" Liam asked. Had more flashes of memory occurred?

"Ever since I've been back I've felt this overwhelming sense of familiarity. I can't put my finger on anything in particular—but it's there, right under the surface."

Liam felt his heart pound like crazy inside his chest. His feelings about Ruby's memories were so conflicted. He desperately wanted her to get her remembrances back, but at the same time he dreaded what she might remember about the state of their marriage. It was a selfish thought, he realized, considering all Aidan stood to gain if Ruby was whole again.

"Where are you staying tonight? If you like, I can put you in our guest room," Liam offered.

"I have a reservation at the B and B on Jarvis Street." She twiddled her fingers and looked down. "I'll only be staying there for two nights, Liam. Then I've got to catch my flight back home."

Home? What was Ruby talking about? Love, Alaska, was her home, whether she realized it or not yet. He believed that with a deep certainty, despite his doubts about his relationship with his wife.

"Why don't you let me cancel your reservation?" he suggested. "Stay here with us. You'll be able to spend more quality time with Aidan in his element."

Ruby regarded him solemnly and then nodded her agreement. "I know that I only just met him, but he's everything you said he was." She glanced over at their son. "I don't need my memory back to tell me that he's the best thing I've ever done in this world."

"I feel the same way," he said as a feeling of pride swept over him.

Aidan patted the seat next to him then beckoned Ruby with his other hand. "Come sit with me," he called out, clearly wanting to be near and dear with his mother.

As he watched her settle next to Aidan at the table,

Liam's thoughts were focused on his son's quality of life. Aidan needed his mother. His son's world would be so much richer with her in it. How many times had Aidan cried himself to sleep because he didn't have a mother? Or asked him dozens of questions about Ruby? There were so many things that only a woman could provide for a young boy. A tender touch. A lullaby to put him to sleep. A soft place to fall when he needed it.

This was all about Aidan. For the moment Liam wasn't even putting himself in the equation. His own heart had been a little bit broken when Ruby had taken off her rings and headed to Colorado on the rescue mission. And even though he was ecstatic about her return, he still felt as if he was walking on a tightrope. What if Ruby remembered that she had asked for a separation? What if he did what he had always done with Ruby and followed his heart, only to have it smashed to pieces again?

No, he wasn't going down that road. His one and only goal would be to give his son his most fervent Christmas wish. The best gift God could ever bestow on him. A mother of his own.

Chapter Four

Ruby woke the next morning with the smell of bacon wafting under her nose. She sat up in bed and cast a quick glance around her. She had been so exhausted last night after all the Prescotts had left the house that she'd barely had time to take in her surroundings.

The guest bedroom had a quaint, cozy vibe. An oil painting of the Alaskan tundra hung from the wall. A big, fluffy, eiderdown comforter had kept her warm and cozy all night. The bed frame was made of cedar wood. She had no idea how she recognized the wood, but she did. She reached out and touched its smooth surface as a feeling of familiarity ran through her. Someone had made this for them! A man. One she dearly loved. A face flashed before her eyes—warm brown eyes and a cocoa complexion. An endearing smile and a hearty laugh. Her brother?

Before she had turned in, Aidan had peeked into her room and wished her good-night. He had been a little shy but filled with curiosity about her. She was so worried about disappointing him. Ruby fretted that in his mind she was a super hero. That would be a tough act to follow.

She quickly got dressed and checked her appearance in the mirror above the dresser. In her baby blue sweater and jeans, she appeared casual and not half as serious as she felt. A slight case of nerves overtook her. For all intents and purposes, she was a stranger in her own home. Aidan and Liam were blank slates for her. Yet every time she looked at her son she felt a tugging sensation in the region of her heart. Try as she might to convince herself that he was a stranger to her, he made her feel things she hadn't ever felt before. Or at least not since she'd woken up as an amnesiac.

Once she left the bedroom, the delectable aromas of breakfast food emanating from the kitchen were even more enticing. Before she had even managed to take a step, Aidan stood from his spot on the floor outside her door. Right next to him was a fire engine set he'd been playing with as he'd waited. He sent her a smile that made her heart do flip-flops.

"Daddy said I should let you sleep."

"That was mighty nice of him," Ruby said, stuffing her hands into the pockets of her jeans.

Big brown eyes that looked a lot like her own gazed up at her. "Are you hungry? We're having bacon and flapjacks."

She rubbed her tummy and let out a contented sigh. "Bacon. I love bacon."

"Me, too," he said, his voice ripe with enthusiasm.

She winked at her son. "And flapjacks ain't so bad, either."

"Daddy made them specially for you. And I helped stir the batter."

"That's wonderful. I always say it's all in the stirring." She smiled at him, noticing the way he was staring at her with a hopeful expression on his face. She felt a burst of sympathy for him. He was so little. Way too young to wrap his head around his mother unceremoniously showing up in his life after having been presumed dead for two years. She wished there was a manual for how to deal with this situation with grace and wisdom. As it was, she felt scared to death about saying or doing the wrong thing.

She bent at the waist and peered into his perfect little face. "Is there anything you want to ask me?"

Aidan shifted from one foot to the other. "How can you be my mother if you don't remember me?" His lips quivered.

Aw. It was a sucker punch straight to the gut.

She swallowed past the lump in her throat. "Well, unfortunately, due to my accident, there are lots of memories I can't access. And I may not remember everything about you, but I do recall certain things."

His eyes widened. "You do? Like what?"

"Smells. I can't be around talcum powder without thinking about holding a baby in my arms. One who had dark hair and chubby little legs. That was you, Aidan."

His jaw dropped. "Wow. That's so cool. Daddy showed me a picture once of you holding me like that when I was a baby. Maybe he can find it so I can show you. It might help you remember more things."

Tears misted her eyes. His voice was filled with such hope and innocence. She prayed he didn't get hurt in all of this. There was still so much to sort out. How would Aidan react when she left to go back to Colorado? Was he imagining that his parents would reunite and live happily-ever-after? As an almost-five-year-old it was entirely possible.

"I'd like that very much," she murmured, overcome with emotion.

"After we eat, can I show you my Christmas list I made for Santa?"

She reached out and palmed his cheek, shocking herself by the intimate gesture. "Sure, Aidan. That would be great."

"Let's eat before the flapjacks get cold." He reached for her hand and tugged her down the hall into the kitchen. Once she crossed the threshold, she stopped in her tracks. Liam was standing at the stove, looking impossibly handsome in a pair of dark jeans and a long-sleeved, oatmeal-colored shirt. Although she had noted her husband's good looks immediately upon meeting him, she couldn't help but notice that he looked even more handsome today. With his dark brown hair, rugged physique and ice-blue eyes, he was a looker. It was no small wonder she had fallen in love with him and sealed the deal with a ring and a wedding. He was definitely an Alaskan hottie.

"Good morning," he said, spatula in hand as he

flipped the flapjacks on the griddle. "I hope you had a good night's rest."

"I slept like a log," Ruby admitted. "It must be the Alaskan air."

Liam nodded. "I was born and bred in Love, so I'm a little biased about the benefits of this little town."

She shifted from one foot to the other then jammed her hands into the back pockets of her jeans. "Is there anything I can do to help?"

"Not a thing. I'm just about done. Why don't you and Aidan sit down at the table?" Liam nodded in Aidan's direction. "Put some napkins by each place setting, okay?"

Aidan quickly placed the napkins on the table and beamed as if he knew he'd done a good job. Liam walked over and placed platters of flapjacks, bacon and eggs on the table.

As they dug into the breakfast Liam had prepared, Ruby found herself surprised by the lack of awkwardness between the three of them. Strangely enough, she didn't feel nearly as uncomfortable as she usually did in the presence of people. Aidan entertained them with stories about his friends and a little girl down the road who wanted to marry him.

Liam and Ruby exchanged a smile as Aidan explained very solemnly that he didn't have any plans to settle down until he was a grown-up. As soon as he finished eating, Aidan asked to be excused, then jumped up from the table, placed his plate in the sink and ran toward his bedroom.

Liam shook his head, his gaze trailing after their son. "If I had half his energy, I'd be over the moon."

The sound of Liam's laughter washed over her like a warm blanket. It tugged at something deep inside her. She knew his laugh. The deep, throaty sound of it was familiar. It was as if she'd always known it.

She couldn't escape the fact that being back here in Love was stirring up her memories. It hadn't even been a full twenty-four hours and she'd remembered several meaningful things. Perhaps being here was the healing balm she needed.

"I remembered something…or someone," she blurted. "It happened this morning when I woke up."

"You did?" Liam asked, his handsome face lit with surprise.

"Yes," she said with a nod. "This might sound like an odd question, but did someone close to us make the bed in the guest room?"

Liam chuckled. "Someone very near and dear to your heart. Your brother. In addition to being a volunteer fireman, he's also a very skilled woodworker. He made that for us when we moved into this house. It was his creative way of presenting us with a housewarming gift."

Ruby clapped her hands together. "I knew it! His face came to mind, and it was such a vivid recollection. He had this huge smile and it gave me such a good feeling about him."

"Being here seems to have triggered your memories."

"It's pretty staggering, but I would have to agree with you," Ruby said. "As we were flying over Kachemak Bay, this feeling of familiarity began to gnaw at me. The moment the seaplane landed in Love, I got goose bumps." She shivered at the recollection then wrapped her arms around her middle. "There was this feeling of déjà vu. I knew I'd been here before even though I didn't have specific memories to ground me. It was palpable."

Liam stared at her, his eyes assessing. "I know you hadn't planned on staying in Love, but now that you know about Aidan…would you consider staying in town for a while so the two of you can work on rebuilding your relationship?"

Even though it was the last thing she'd expected to hear, a feeling of calm settled over her. Love, Alaska, was so lovely and quaint and unlike anything she'd known in Denver. Was it possible that she might find roots in this quaint fishing village? In coming here, her sole goal had been to discover her identity. Naively, she had imagined that once she dug up her past she would return to Denver. Finding out about her family had changed everything. God had other plans for her. She knew He had planted her exactly where she needed to be.

Aidan belonged to her. And for the last two years, there hadn't been a single person or place she'd felt this way about. It was love—primal, gut-wrenching love that emanated from her very core. What she felt for her son surpassed anything else she might feel about the situation. It was still nerve-racking, and she was still afraid, but she wanted to see things through in Love. Ruby wanted to build relationships rather than fumble through life without any meaningful connections.

There were still a few questions rattling around inside her head. "How would that work, Liam? What about my job?" Even though her waitressing gig was no great shakes, she depended on it for income.

"If you're worried about money, I'll write you a check for the money that was in your savings account. After you were officially declared deceased, the monies were transferred over to my account." He scratched his jaw. For the first time she noticed a slight five-o'clock shadow. It only served to make him more ruggedly attractive. "And I've been holding on to the majority of your personal belongings—clothes, jewelry, toiletries." He made a face. "The thought of getting rid of everything seemed too final."

"That's understandable. It would have made it too final, I imagine." Sadness swept over her at the thought of Liam having to perform that solemn duty. He seemed like such a strong man, but it spoke volumes about his grief that two years in and he hadn't been able to dispose of her belongings.

"We're going to have to contact the authorities so they can reverse their declaration about your status. That way you can get an Alaskan driver's license and credit cards with your name on them."

"I have a Colorado driver's license. When I lived with Trudy and Ezra they let me tool around with their car. I figured out pretty quickly that I knew how to drive."

"You learned to drive at fifteen," Liam explained. "An accomplishment that you were quite proud of. Your father showed you the ropes."

Her father. Other than a feeling of happiness when she thought of her childhood, there still wasn't much of a memory of him. Or her mother. It saddened her, particularly since they were no longer living. She would never have the opportunity to see them again or share her life with them.

"So, if I decide to stay in Love for a period of time, how would it play out between us?" She fumbled with how to express herself. "I know we're still married, so I'm just wondering."

She wasn't sure if he would expect her to work on their relationship, as well. After all, they were husband and wife. Did he still love her? Would her feelings for Liam come back to her in one fell swoop?

"I don't have any more answers about our marriage than you do, if that's what you're asking. There'll be plenty of time in the future to figure that out. For now, Aidan comes first. That's where our focus should be."

She let out a relieved breath. Working on a marriage when she didn't remember her husband would have been extremely difficult. Not to mention awkward. Now if she could just stop staring at the little cleft in his chin and his wide shoulders.

"I know it might not be easy to leave your job and friends behind for an extended period, but I think we can both agree that our son's needs should come before anything else."

Ruby shrugged. "My life in Denver is…small. I don't have a large circle of friends. And my job…well, let's just say that I'm not saving lives the way you do. It's not the stuff of which dreams are made." She bowed her head, feeling embarrassed at what she'd just revealed.

Before she knew it, Liam's fingers were at her chin,

lifting it so that their eyes were level. Compassion flared in his eyes. "Hey. Don't down yourself. You've been on a torturous journey these last few years. I can't even imagine how difficult your life has been. And it strikes me that you're just as brave as you've always been. You may not have been saving lives on rescue missions for the past two years, but you've been putting one foot in front of the other and surviving. That's huge."

They looked into each other's eyes as an electric pulse crackled in the air around them. Her eyes shifted to his lips. They were full and perfectly shaped. What would it be like to be kissed by this tender, giving man? It was sad that she couldn't remember what it felt like to be kissed. Or to be held by someone who loved her. She let out a sigh. Sometimes it felt as if those days were behind her.

"I want Aidan to have a mother," Liam said in a strangled voice.

She fiddled with her fingers. "I do, too, but I don't know how to be that. I'm going to have to learn how all over again." Even though the thought of it was terrifying, it was also invigorating. Heartwarming. Being someone's mother gave her a purpose in life outside of herself. For the last two years there hadn't been anything that inspired or motivated her. She had basically been putting one foot in front of the other and trudging through life. That wasn't living! It was merely existing.

"I promise to help you, Ruby. Can we work something out that doesn't involve you going back to Colorado, at least not yet? Give Love a chance. Maybe you'll find you like it here." The look on Liam's face could only be described as intense. "Please? For Aidan?"

She ran a shaky hand through her long brown tresses. Staring into his eyes for too long made her feel nervous. It seemed impossible to resist his plea when he appeared to be motivated by love and concern for Aidan.

"Where would I live?" she asked. She couldn't imagine herself living all by her lonesome in strange surroundings. One thing she had learned about herself since the accident was that she didn't thrive well in solitary settings. She needed human contact.

Liam gestured around him with his hands. "I'd like it if you would stay here with us. There's plenty of room. Honor was staying with us, but she just moved to live out at the wildlife center. I think it's the perfect venue for you to bond with Aidan and get your bearings."

The idea of living with Liam and Aidan in this fairy-tale house nestled in the Alaskan woods was appealing. It was far nicer than anything she'd experienced in the last few years. She could put her cooking skills to use in this airy, fantastic kitchen. And she would be close to her son…and Liam, too. The idea of spending time around her husband was a bit nerve-racking. She didn't want to get pulled under by the sheer force of his magnetism. There was so much to figure out and process. Would he expect her to fall into old, familiar rhythms she didn't even remember? Was he hoping to get his partner back?

"I think being here is helping me to recover my lost memories, which is why I came here in the first place. Sticking around for my son is a no-brainer. There's really no way I can say no."

Liam let out a huge sigh that sounded like relief. He reached out and placed his hand over hers. He gently squeezed it. Ruby felt a spark in response. Liam's eyes widened as if he had also felt a connection. Judging by his expression, he was just as surprised as she was by it.

Just then Aidan darted into the room. His hair appeared less rumpled, and he had changed out of his pajamas into a pair of corduroys and a festive sweater. "Hey, Dad. Remember you said we were going to pick out our tree today."

Liam let out a groan. "It's amazing how you can remember all of my promises, yet you keep forgetting to brush your teeth before bed."

Ruby giggled at the sight of Aidan jumping up and down with excitement. She hoped she would be able to keep up with him and his unbridled enthusiasm and energy.

"Hey, buddy, I'm on call today, so I have to be ready to run to the clinic if anyone needs me. You know the drill, right?"

Aidan nodded his head. "Yep. You made a sacred oath to help people."

"That's my boy," Liam said, his tone full of pride.

Aidan walked over to his dad and tugged at his sleeve. He gestured for him to lean down. Aidan cupped his hands around his mouth and began whispering loudly in his father's ear. Ruby couldn't hear every word, but she managed to overhear the words "tree" and "please" and "ask." Suddenly, two pairs of eyes were focused on her.

"Ask her," Aidan urged in a loud whisper. He put his finger in his mouth and began to nibble.

"How about it, Ruby?" Liam asked. "Do you want to come with us into town and go shopping for an Alaskan Christmas tree?"

Watching Ruby getting along with Aidan like a house on fire warmed Liam's insides like nothing else ever could. They had driven into town and parked on Jarvis Street, then made their way to the town green where Alan Pendergast's tree stand had been set up. Liam's family had been buying trees from Mr. Pendergast ever since he could remember. Now, he was passing the tradition down to his own son.

This moment was almost surreal. If anyone had told him two days ago that he'd be picking out a Christmas tree with Ruby and his son today, he would have called them all kinds of crazy. God was good! He had given his family back the person who had always been at the core of it with her huge heart and unwavering kindness.

A tight feeling seized his chest as he studied the familiar, graceful slope of Ruby's neck and the long strands of mahogany hair that trailed down past her shoulders. A hint of a smile played around her lips. She was patiently listening to Aidan and nodding her head in response to his comments.

Was the woman he loved still in there somewhere? Was she still his Ruby? Or had all that changed forever as a result of her head trauma?

Ruby had always been the love of his life. They had planned on being each other's forever. He fought against a feeling of sadness that crept over him. So much had changed between them. Ruby didn't even remember him, which he was trying not to take personally. She remembered Aidan and Kyle and the town of Love, as well as a host of other important things. But not him. Not a single memory of him or all the happy times they had shared. It played into every insecurity he had about his relationship with his wife. And even though he dreaded her remembering the rocky state of their marriage at the time of her accident, he still ached to have her remember the sweet and tender moments—their wedding, Aidan's birth, their very first Christmas together as man and wife.

He stuffed down the feelings of hurt. This wasn't about him. Aidan was the focus here. Sooner or later he and Ruby would have to figure out where they were headed, but for now it was all about restoring Aidan's relationship with Ruby. It would be the ultimate Christmas gift.

As he watched Aidan, Liam had the sneaking suspicion his son's face might crack under the weight of his huge grin. Liam felt as if his heart had expanded to ten times its normal size just watching his joy. It pulsed and hummed in the frigid December air. Aidan was on top of the world as he walked hand in hand with Ruby. Every time he saw an appealing tree, he would begin circling it and eyeing it up and down.

Although word had gotten around about Ruby's return, there was still a good amount of heads turning in their direction, as well as astonished faces. Thankfully, the place was fairly deserted. Otherwise it would have been overwhelming for Ruby. And Liam was a little tired of explaining the situation to the few townsfolk who pulled him aside and asked. He didn't blame them for being shocked, but he simply wanted to savor this moment with his family. Liam felt fairly certain his grandfather might have to call a town meeting simply to announce the incredible news.

His family. He still couldn't believe it. Tears misted his eyes. He blinked them away before Aidan or Ruby could see them.

"This one!" Aidan said triumphantly as he pointed at a large pine tree. "Isn't it great, Dad?"

Liam walked over and looked the tree up and down. He turned toward Ruby, who had a bemused expression on her face. "It's pretty impressive. What do you think?"

"I think it's a keeper," Ruby said, holding her palm up so Aidan could give her a high-five. He jumped up and slapped her hand, letting out an enthusiastic cry that sounded a lot like triumph.

"If you're sure, I can go pay Mr. Pendergast," Liam said. Aidan gave him a thumbs-up sign.

Liam paid for the tree and helped Al carry it over to his truck where they strapped it down with rope.

Once the tree was secure, Aidan seized the moment. "Can we go to the Moose Café for hot chocolate? I want to show my m..." His voice trailed off after he stumbled with the words.

Ruby bent and tweaked his nose. "It's all right to call me Mom. If you want to," she said. She glanced over at Liam with a questioning look in her eyes.

Liam sent her an encouraging nod. He hadn't thought to bring up this topic before. Calling her Mom would be natural, but perhaps it would be too much too soon for Aidan.

"I don't want to hurt your feelings," Aidan said, his eyes focused on the snowy ground, "but it might take a while to get used to. So I might wait a while. If that's okay with you?" He didn't look up at Ruby but began to push the snow around with the tip of his boot.

"Of course it is," Ruby said in a gentle voice. "I'm sort of relieved that you said that because, if I'm being completely honest with you, Aidan, it's going to take a little bit for me to get used to being your mother. And I hope that doesn't hurt your feelings, because as far as I can see, you're the most awesome almost-five-year-old on the planet."

Aidan tried to keep it together but his grin was effusive. Liam let out a sigh of relief. There were bound to be bumps and hiccups on the road ahead, but it was comforting to know that Ruby and Aidan had worked this one out on their own. There would be plenty of time for Aidan to get used to his mother on his own terms and at a pace that felt comfortable to him.

"How does hot chocolate sound?" Liam asked with a glance in Ruby's direction.

Ruby bobbed her head. "It sounds perfect." She held up her mittened hands. "My fingers are beginning to tingle. This material is no match for Alaska cold. I need to invest in a new pair of mittens."

"There's also lattes and mochaccinos and tea and lots of other types of coffee drinks." Aidan practically chirped. "This place aims to please."

"Wow," Ruby said. "You're good! You could be a great advertisement for the Moose Café."

"Cameron has been training him well," Liam teased, patting Aidan on top of his hat-covered head.

They all chuckled, with Aidan laughing louder than either of them. As they walked down Jarvis Street, pausing to admire the festively decorated store windows, Liam wondered if anything felt familiar to Ruby. He stopped himself from asking her, realizing that it might get tiresome to have to continually answer questions about her memories.

Before he knew it, they were standing in front of his brother's establishment. The bronze, embellished sign welcomed them to the Moose Café, Love's most happening coffee bar. "We might as well bite the bullet and go inside," Liam said. He sucked in a strengthening breath of air.

"Is it going to be that bad?" Ruby fretted.

Liam made a face. "Um, how should I put this? You were beloved in this town. Still are."

She raised an eyebrow. "Which is a good thing," Ruby said. "Right?"

"Yes. But that means that there are dozens and dozens of villagers who are going to go a little bit crazy when they see you. Not to mention all the members of my family who are going to swarm all over you, like Cameron and Paige…and then there's Hazel, and Declan and his new wife, Annie. Not to mention Sophie and Myrtle."

Ruby's eyes bulged. She made a gulping sound. "Wow. Sounds like I had a lot of friends."

"Sophie and Annie are new to town. They both came as part of the Operation Love program. But everybody who knew you, loved you." Liam's statement hung in the air, dangling like a fully inflated balloon. *Especially me.* He almost blurted it out but he stopped himself. It wasn't the time or the place to go down that road. At the moment it would only serve to muddy the waters.

"No matter how crazy it gets, don't forget I'm here. I've got your back," Liam said.

He opened the door to the café, allowing Aidan to sail through as if he owned the place. Try as he might, Liam couldn't stop himself from wanting to protect his wife. He placed his hand on her lower back and ushered her inside, all the while praying she would be able to handle her re-entry into Love society.

Chapter Five

The moment Ruby stepped inside the Moose Café, delectable aromas assailed her senses. Aidan ran off toward the kitchen as if his sneakers were on fire. Waitresses with cartoon moose emblazoned on their T-shirts hustled to and fro, serving customers and taking orders. There was a loud din emanating from the robust crowd. Perhaps it served as an indication of the popularity of this particular establishment. It was filled to capacity. A roasting fire roared in the dining area, lending a rustic, warm atmosphere to the eatery. Antlers hung on the wall above the fireplace.

She heard several people call out to Liam. "Hey, Dr. Prescott" and "I need to see you about my gout."

The place oozed charm. It seemed like the sort of eatery where you could settle in for a refreshing coffee and good conversation while enjoying a pleasant ambience.

"Liam!" a boisterous voice called out. Ruby turned to see a tall, good-looking man with dark hair and an easy stride making his way toward them. He exuded a great deal of confidence. He flashed them a pearly smile.

"Welcome to the Moose Café, Ruby. Let me show you to a place of honor at my best table over here." He held out his elbow so she could place her arm through it. The gentlemanly gesture made her want to chuckle. He was treating her like a fragile piece of china.

Liam glared at the man. "Cameron. Take it down a few notches, okay?"

"Sorry," Cameron said in a less animated voice. He reached out and grabbed Ruby by the hand. He raised her hand to his lips and pressed a kiss against her knuckles. "I can't tell you how overjoyed we all are that you've come back to us."

Aw. He was a sweetheart in addition to being almost as gorgeous as Liam. This town sure had its fair share of attractive men. No wonder the media was in a frenzy over this town's matchmaking program. It was just the type of human interest story that you read about in glossy magazines.

"In case you haven't figured it out yet, this is my brother, Cameron. He's the owner of this place," Liam explained.

"Nice to see you, Cameron. Your café is gorgeous," Ruby said. "And if the aroma is any indication, I know I'm going to enjoy the food here."

"Thanks. My wife, Paige, helped me redecorate it. Let's just say it was a little masculine in its décor. That's what happens when you have a town full of men."

"Ruby." A sweet, feminine voice washed over them. A tall, regal woman with blond hair and a stunning face took faltering steps toward her. She stopped short, seeming to be wary of crossing any boundaries. "I know you don't remember us, but I'm Paige. We were best friends."

"Hi, Paige," Ruby said, wishing she could remember this woman who had clearly been an important part of her life. A sudden sound caused her to look down. A beautiful little girl who looked a lot like Cameron stood clutching her mother's leg. She looked up at Ruby with curious, almond-shaped eyes. Then she gifted her with a toothy grin that melted Ruby's heart.

By this time all the patrons were staring and whispering. It made her feel uncomfortable. Ruby moved closer to Liam. It felt awkward to be the topic of everyone's conversation, especially when none of the faces were even remotely familiar. Why had she agreed to come inside the café in the first place? She felt completely outside her comfort zone.

"As I live and breathe!" A tall, broad-shouldered woman with graying hair stepped into their circle. An apron decorated with dancing moose let Ruby know she was one of Cameron's employees. Tears streamed down her face and she wiped them away with the back of her hand. "Jasper told me you were among the living, but a part of me couldn't wrap my head around it. Ruby Prescott, you're a sight for sore eyes. Come over here and give me some sugar." The woman held her arms open wide and motioned for Ruby to step toward her. When Ruby hesitantly approached her, she felt strong arms envelope her. Helpless to extricate herself, Ruby sank into the embrace.

All of a sudden, a sharp, high-pitched whistle brought silence to the room. Ruby found herself being tugged away from the embrace. Mayor Jasper Prescott was standing there with an irate expression stamped on his craggy face. His cheeks were rosy, although Ruby wasn't certain if it was from the frigid temperatures outside or his ire.

"Hazel, give the gal some breathing room!" Jasper barked. "You're going to suffocate her with all that mothering you're doing."

"Oh, give it a rest, Jasper," Hazel fumed. "We were having a moment until you came barreling in here like an out-of-control tornado."

"If you'd have hugged her any tighter she might have snapped in two." Jasper huffed. "Let the girl get acclimated before you start squeezing the life out of her."

Hazel let out a harrumphing sound and turned her back on Jasper. "Neanderthal," she muttered. She turned all of her attention back to Ruby. "Welcome back, darling," Hazel said, wiping away tears from her face. "I know you don't remember me, but we were almost like family. Before you married your honey here, you lived out at my Black Bear cabins. Those sure were some good times. I'm looking forward to making new memories with you."

All Ruby could do was smile. Her face felt a little stiff from grinning. She didn't know what else to do in response to all the love the townsfolk were showing her. Her head was beginning to spin. She now knew what Liam had been referring to earlier when he'd been hesitant to enter the café. She would never have imagined that a tiny fishing village could have so much of a social component. Granted it was almost lunchtime, but the

Moose Café was a real whirlwind. People were coming out of the woodwork.

She could feel the heat of Liam's gaze. He narrowed his eyes and studied her then leaned in toward her. "Are you all right?" he asked in a tender voice. "Just say the word and we can blow this Popsicle stand."

"I'll be fine once we sit down and order a hot cocoa," she said in a low voice. "I'd like to get off my feet."

Liam turned toward Hazel. "Hey, can you find us a table?"

"Why don't you sit down at this table right here and I'll make you the best hot chocolate known to mankind," Hazel suggested. Her eyes radiated kindness. "Aidan is in the back with Sophie, by the way. She's showing him how to make frozen hot chocolate."

"While you're back there, make me one of those caramel lattes with the cinnamon sprinkled on top," Jasper requested.

Hazel let out a snort. "Coming right up, Your Highness. One caramel latte sprinkled with arsenic flavoring."

As she stomped away, Jasper frowned at her retreating figure. He shook his head. "You heard that, right? Threatening the life of a beloved town leader."

"Jasper, be nice," Paige cautioned. "You've really been sniping at Hazel lately. A woman can only take so much." She bent and picked up her daughter, then handed her to Cameron.

Jasper sputtered. "That right there is a perfect example of why I'm not putting a ring on it." He began muttering under his breath. “Plenty of women would be mighty glad to have a boyfriend like me.”

“Yeah,” Cameron said. “Those Operation Love gals are just lining up outside the mayor’s office in droves, aren’t they?”

Liam rolled his eyes. “Don’t mind Hazel and Jasper. They have a love tiff at least once a week.” He pulled out the chair so Ruby could sit.

“I figured they might be romantically involved by the way they were bantering. They’re both pretty feisty,” Ruby remarked. “For a moment I thought we might have to take cover.”

“Just so you know, you and Liam weren’t like that,” Cameron interjected. “I promise. You were the perfect couple as far as this town was concerned. Ruby and Liam forever.”

Liam jabbed his brother in the side. Cameron made a grunting sound then shot Liam a dirty look.

Perfect couple? Just hearing that phrase made Ruby feel she had a lot to live up to. The word “perfect” rubbed her the wrong way. And although she knew Cameron was only trying to be complimentary, it made her feel that there was no way she could ever be half as wonderful as the Ruby she’d once been. It wasn’t possible. She was no longer that woman. And even if she got her memory back, she’d be a different woman than the one who had left this town two years ago. Suddenly it felt like she would be trying to fit into a life that no longer existed as it once had been.

“Attention, please. Attention.” Jasper scrambled up on a chair and let loose with another whistle to get everyone's attention. He was wildly waving his arms around.

"Unbelievable!" Liam muttered as he folded his arms across his chest and sat back in his chair.

"If he breaks that chair, he's paying for it," Cameron grumbled. "There's no family discount for destroying the property around here."

As soon as all eyes were focused on Jasper, he began to speak. "I'd like to make an announcement. I'm sure most of you are pretty confused about what's been happening here today. The Prescott family is delighted to announce that reports of Ruby Prescott's death were greatly exaggerated." He let out a chuckle. "Not that it's anything to make light of, but we're just so thankful to have her back in the fold."

Loud gasps and murmurs rippled through the café. Customers turned toward her to gape at her. Ruby ducked her head. She didn't want to make eye contact with anyone. Awkward didn't even begin to describe this experience. She might have liked some warning about Jasper's announcement, but one look at Liam's face told her he'd been caught off guard, as well.

"Ruby has amnesia, but God has shown Ruby the way home after two years. She was in an accident that day in Colorado when she was saving lives. As a result, she's lost most of her memory of life before that day. That means that in all likelihood she won't remember you. It also means that we're going to help her in any way that we can. With patience. And kindness. And good, old-fashioned Alaskan hospitality. She still has healing to do on her road to recovery. This town has always supported our own and this won't be any different."

"Hear! Hear! Mayor Prescott!" Hazel stood nearby, clapping and cheering. Ruby spotted Aidan standing nearby, beaming from ear to ear. A stunning redhead—presumably Sophie—had her arm around his shoulder. Hazel stepped forward and helped Jasper down from the chair, then reached out and grazed her palm along his cheek. "That's the Jasper I know and love," she cooed.

"And don't you forget it, woman," Jasper said as he reached for Hazel and placed his arms around her waist, then dipped her backward as he planted a kiss on her lips.

"Close your eyes, Emma," Cameron said to his baby daughter as he placed his hand over her eyes. "You really don't need to see this."

Paige reached over and removed his hand from their daughter's eyes. She shook her head at her husband and made a tutting sound.

Everyone in the Moose Café began clapping and hooting. Liam threw back his head and laughed. It was nice to see him so relaxed and lighthearted, Ruby realized. It suited him well.

Ruby felt shame almost eat her up inside as she watched Hazel and Jasper's display of affection. When the town mayor had first begun to speak, she'd wanted to sink into her seat. She had felt embarrassed and slightly annoyed. Jasper's words had surprised her. They'd been heartwarming and beautiful, leaving her feeling choked-up. Since she was struggling to discover what her place was in this Alaskan town, it meant the world to her to know that she had his support and friendship.

God had led her back here to Love. Of that she felt certain. Now if she could only figure out her role in the grand scheme of things.

Aidan's mother. Liam's wife. Friend to all.

Those things were meaningful, but were they enough to keep her in this town for the long haul when she still didn't remember much of anything about her former life?

Not long after Aidan joined them for hot chocolate at the table, Liam could detect fatigue etched on Ruby's face. Her warm brown skin seemed a bit washed out, and her eyes no longer sparkled. She appeared a bit worn down. He chided himself for indulging Aidan in his desire to have hot chocolate at the Moose Café. He feared it had been too overwhelming an experience for Ruby. Between Jasper, Cameron, Paige and Hazel, not to mention a handful of villagers who had approached Ruby with well wishes, it had turned into a lot more than a casual outing. He imagined Ruby felt as if she was being pulled in a dozen different directions.

After saying their goodbyes, Liam drove them back to the house. Ruby was very quiet during the ride. He tried to lighten the mood by turning the radio on and blasting festive holiday songs. Aidan played along, singing his favorites at the top of his lungs. Although he saw Ruby tapping along to the beat a few times, she remained somber. From this point forward he vowed to do a better job of protecting Ruby from situations that were too much for her to handle.

As he navigated the lane and pulled into the driveway, a familiar physique standing at their doorstep immediately captured his attention.

"Oh, no. Not now of all times," he muttered.

Ruby turned toward him, her brown eyes full of concern. "What is it? Is something wrong?"

"It's Uncle Kyle," Aidan shouted. As soon as the truck came to a stop, he quickly unbuckled his seat belt and wrenched open the door.

"Kyle? Isn't that my brother's name?" Ruby asked. Her pretty features were creased with worry. "Is that him?"

"Yes," Liam said in a clipped tone. Frustration speared through him. Already, Ruby was feeling overwhelmed by the events of this afternoon. He'd told Kyle to call him so they could arrange a time for him to come visit Ruby. Clearly, Kyle had decided to just fly to Love from Homer.

Ruby bit her lip. "He's a big guy. If the fireman thing doesn't work out, he may have a future in professional wrestling."

Ruby's comment made Liam grin. At six-three and two hundred and twenty-five pounds, Kyle was known as a gentle giant. Well-mannered and kind, he was a favorite among the townsfolk here in Love whenever he visited. Aidan thought he was the very definition of cool.

Liam and Ruby emerged from the vehicle and headed toward the house. Kyle was holding Aidan in his arms, but his stare was intently focused on Ruby. Tears welled in his eyes. He slowly lowered Aidan to the ground.

Before Liam could say a word, Kyle stepped toward Ruby. "I know you're not expecting me, but I couldn't stay away. I've been missing you for two long years, and not seeing you for another single day felt like torture."

"I understand," Ruby said in a low voice. She was gazing at her brother with such intensity it seemed almost as if she was trying to memorize his facial features.

"I know you don't remember me—" Kyle began.

"That's not true," Ruby said with a vehement shake of her head. "I do remember you. Your face. Your warm brown eyes. A smile like no other. I have a distinct recollection of you crafting that bed in the guest room for us. And jelly beans."

Tears slid down Kyle's face. "You do remember me."

Ruby reached up and wrapped her arms around Kyle. She placed her head against his chest and closed her eyes.

Jelly Bean was the nickname Ruby had given Kyle when he was a kid, due to his effusive love for jelly beans.

Liam didn't know if he'd ever felt as jealous before in his life than he did at this very moment. Ruby had distinct memories of Kyle! And she had reached out to him with an embrace. He swallowed past the huge lump in his throat. It wasn't a contest, but knowing that she still had no recollection of him or their life together burned like acid.

It served as a huge reminder that the love Ruby had once felt for him had in all likelihood died even before she'd tumbled off the Colorado mountain.

* * *

Liam and Kyle took the tree down from the top of the truck and carried it into the house. All the while Aidan was shouting out directions. Ruby trailed after them, excited at the idea of an honest-to-goodness, live pine tree for Christmas. Last year she'd put up a little plastic tree that had resembled something out of a cartoon. Things were definitely looking up!

"Where would you like it, Ruby?" Liam asked. "It's your choice."

Ruby looked around the living room. There was a great spot right in front of the window that would be perfect. "Right there by the window," she said, pointing over at it. "That way anyone who comes to visit can see the tree all lit up from the outside."

She didn't know where that idea had come from. It had just popped into her head. She could see it all in her mind—the tree fully adorned with strings of lights and popcorn and cranberries. Precious ornaments handed down from family members would hang gracefully from the branches. A gold star shimmering brightly from the top.

Aidan grabbed the Christmas tree stand and placed it on the floor directly in front of the huge bay window. Kyle lifted the tree and placed it into the hold while Liam got down on the floor and began tightening the screws so the tree would stay up.

"There we go," Liam said as he scrambled to his feet and eyed the tree. "It looks straight, right?"

"As straight as an arrow," Ruby remarked. "It looks wonderful."

"I can't wait to decorate it," Aidan shouted, jumping up and down with excitement. "This year Daddy said he's going to lift me up so I can put the star on top."

The sound of a cell phone buzzing caused Liam to dig around in his pockets. He pulled out the phone and said, "I've got to take this. It's the answering service for the clinic." He strode out of the room and walked in the direction of the kitchen.

"Uncle Kyle, wait right here. I need to go get my new fireman truck so I can show you." Like a flash, Aidan disappeared right before their eyes.

Suddenly it was just the two of them standing there looking at each other as if neither knew how to bridge the gap.

"Would you like something to drink? A snack?" Ruby asked, feeling desperate to fill the silence.

"I'm good. The question is…how are you doing? Really?" He leaned toward her and reached for her hand. Kyle squeezed it gently.

It felt like being supported by a strong oak tree.

She gestured toward the sofa. "Why don't we sit down so we're more comfortable?" Ruby suggested. She sank onto the couch and watched as Kyle sat next to her.

"I'm doing well. Or as well as can be expected. I didn't expect all this when I came to town." She let out a laugh. "I guess I was naive to think that I was going to stroll into town, find my family connections and then just sail out of town back to Denver."

"So how are you handling it all? Aidan and Liam? And all the Prescotts? They can be an intense bunch."

"Everything is coming at me kind of fast right now. I just came from town. We stopped into Cameron's café after picking out our tree. The hustle and bustle and the people quickly became overwhelming." Tears stung her eyes. "I want to be strong enough to face this, but I have to admit, I just wanted to bury my head under my covers."

"And here I just show up unannounced on your doorstep to add to your troubles." Kyle groaned. He slapped his palm on his forehead.

"It's fine," Ruby said. "To tell you the truth, I don't feel overwhelmed at all sitting here with you one-on-one like this. I think the sheer number of people makes me a little uncomfortable."

Kyle nodded, his expression infused with sympathy. "You were a people person. A social butterfly. Ever since you were little, people have been drawn to you. So of course they're flocking to you now, because they all shared a connection with you in the past. And I'm sure that must feel intense to you since all you have is a blank slate."

She sighed with relief. "Yes. You understand it perfectly. And Liam has been fantastic, but it's strange knowing we're husband and wife. Be honest with me, Kyle. How were we as a couple? Liam and I? Were we head-over-heels in love? Was I a good mother?"

These questions had been plaguing her ever since her arrival. She had left her toddler son at home to go on a dangerous search-and-rescue mission in another state. It worried her that perhaps she had been one of those mothers who put her career before her husband and child. If that was the case, she would feel ashamed of her choices.

"First of all, you were a fantastic, engaged mom. From the time Aidan was born, both you and Liam doted on him. First steps. First words. You were both over the moon about him." He let out a ragged breath. "From the moment you met Liam, it was a love story. You fell for each other pretty fast, then got engaged and tied the knot shortly thereafter. Everyone in Love held you up as the gold standard." Kyle held up his hands. "No pressure, though."

Ruby let out a sigh. "That's the problem. I do feel that pressure to be something I can't even begin to wrap my head around. And, of course, Liam is this dreamy doctor with soulful eyes and a good heart, but it's not like I'm in love with him or anything."

A loud crash startled both of them.

Aidan was standing there in the doorway, his red fire truck on its side on the floor. His cheeks were blotchy, fists clenched at his sides. He was huffing and puffing like a fire-breathing dragon. "You don't love my dad? That's awful. Maybe you should just go back to Colorado where you belong!"

Chapter Six

Just as Liam ended his call, the sound of a loud crash drew him back toward the living room. He saw Aidan run down the hall into his bedroom, followed by a loud slam of his door.

"What in the world just happened here?" Liam asked, looking back and forth at Ruby and Kyle. Aidan wasn't a perfect kid by any means, but it wasn't like him to throw temper tantrums.

He spotted the fire truck on the floor in disarray. One of the ladders had broken off, along with a tire.

"Did he do this?" he asked. Aidan knew better than to treat his belongings so frivolously. Jasper had just purchased the fire truck for him.

"Yes, but he was upset about something he overheard. It's all my fault, Liam," Ruby said tearfully.

Kyle patted her on the shoulder. "Just chalk it up to the extraordinary circumstances of the last few days. It's perfectly normal that he's acting out."

"Let me go talk to him and straighten him out," Liam said in a fierce tone.

Ruby jumped up from the sofa. "No, Liam! Please. Let me do it. I'm the one he's angry at. I need to smooth things over so there isn't any awkwardness moving forward."

"Are you sure? He can be a handful when he's riled up," Liam warned.

"If I'm going to get back in the swing of things with my son, I can't avoid the hard stuff."

"Care to tell me what this was all about?" he asked, studying the frantic expression on her face. Something big must have gone down to lead to Aidan's meltdown and the look of distress etched on Ruby's face.

"Later. After I talk to Aidan," she promised. He nodded as she walked down the hall in search of their son.

Once Ruby was safely out of hearing distance, Kyle leaned back into the sofa and let out a massive sigh. "This is a really complicated situation, Liam. It could really explode if you don't tread carefully."

Liam stiffened. He didn't need to be lectured by his brother-in-law. Kyle had no clue how difficult this situation was to navigate. As confused as he was about his new reality, he had to stay positive. "It'll all work out. We're only two days in, Kyle. We need time to adjust as a family."

Kyle's expression hardened. "I'm not sure how long I can keep Ruby in the dark."

Liam crossed his arms over his chest. "About what?"

A sigh slipped past Kyle's lips. "Come on, Liam. We both know that when Ruby left for that rescue mission the two of you were at odds with one another. You were talking separation. She told me everything."

"Marriages go through rough times and people ride them out." He frowned at his brother-in-law. "And after everything that's happened, how would it serve Ruby to have that information?"

Kyle shrugged. "I don't know. But I do know that my sister and I never kept secrets from one another. And this feels like a big, dark secret to me." Kyle's brows were knitted together, his caramel-brown eyes appeared troubled. "Maybe she should know so she can make informed decisions."

"I would never ask you to be dishonest, Kyle. But with Ruby having suffered amnesia and trying to get her bearings here in Love, I just don't think it would be wise to bring up things that might cause distress."

"For Ruby? Or for you?"

Tension hummed in the air between them.

Liam clenched his jaw. He had always gotten along well with Kyle, who was a kind and loyal guy. But he wasn't about to condone his brother-in-law throwing a keg of dynamite on an already explosive situation. He couldn't risk the hurt Aidan would feel if everything fell apart. Or the pain Ruby might feel. Everything may have changed in his world, but he would never stop being his family's protector.

"I've never given you reason to question my motives before, Kyle. My main concern about telling your sister is Aidan. He's over the moon to have his mother back. Let's give them an opportunity to bond without throwing a monkey wrench in the mix."

Kyle nodded. "I'm sorry if I sounded curt or if it appears that I'm sticking my nose where it doesn't belong. I just don't want this to blow up in everybody's faces."

"Neither do I. I promise you that I'm doing everything in my power to make sure Ruby is safe and protected and loved."

Kyle knitted his brows together. "I believe you, but what if she remembers everything, Liam?"

He felt torn about Kyle's question. On one hand, it would be a dream come true. But, if Ruby had total recall, she might decide their marriage had died two years ago. She would realize he hadn't been completely on the up-and-up with her. Although he had done a good job of convincing himself this was mainly about Aidan, he couldn't deny his marriage hung in the balance.

Either way, this was his marriage and he wasn't going to let anyone else determine its fate. "I'll cross that bridge when I come to it," he said, a slight edge to his voice.

"Just make sure that you protect Ruby in the process," Kyle said.

Cold, harsh anger flared inside him. "She's my wife, Kyle. I've always had her best interests at heart. Since the day we pledged our lives to one another, I've always kept that vow. That's never going to change."

For a moment they stared each other down. The tension between them palpable.

All of a sudden Kyle broke the tension by sticking out his hand. Liam reached out and clasped it. Kyle pulled him in for a hug.

"You're a good man, Liam," Kyle said. "And I've always admired you as a husband and father. I just don't want Ruby hurt any more than she's already been."

Kyle was protecting his sister the same way Ruby had always watched over him and kept him out of harm's way after their parents' deaths. It was ironic that Kyle thought his sister would be the one to get hurt in all of this. Because ever since Ruby had taken off her wedding rings and asked for a separation, Liam's own heart had been on life support.

Ruby had been sitting by Aidan's bed for about ten minutes now. At first he hadn't wanted her to come inside his bedroom, but once he'd allowed her entry, he had buried his face in his pillow and refused to talk to her.

Finally, Ruby reached out and gently turned him on his side.

"Hey, buddy. I know you're angry, but acting like this isn't the answer."

Aidan looked at her through red-rimmed, puffy eyes. "Go away. You're just pretending to like me. I heard what you said to Uncle Kyle out there."

"And that upset you."

Aidan sat up and faced her. "Yes. Parents are supposed to love each other."

Ruby bit her lip. How in the world could she explain this so her son would understand it? He was only a little boy. One who seemed very invested in the idea that his parents would walk off into the Alaskan sunset together. She didn't want to break his little heart, but she also didn't want him to invest in a pipe dream.

"Aidan, right here, right now, I'm going to make a promise to you. I'm never going to lie to you. I've been away for two long years. You know all about how I lost my memory, so you have to remember that loving your father isn't something I remember. Love builds over time and I've only been back for two days."

"W-what about me? Do you love me?" His voice trembled. She could see the longing in his eyes, the heartfelt desire to be loved by his mother. It was the most natural thing in the world.

Ruby hesitated for a moment before answering. She wanted to make sure she spoke from the heart. It was strange to acknowledge it, but she did love her son. Her feelings for him were the most natural, powerful emotions known to mankind. It was innate and instinctual. She knew without a doubt that she would sacrifice her own life to save his. Yes, indeed. It was love.

She reached out and tweaked his nose. "Yes, I love you, Aidan. As surely as the moon glows in the night sky, I do."

He scrunched his face up. "Then how come that's different than loving Daddy?"

"For some reason I don't need to have all my memories intact to tell me that what I feel for you is love." She put her arm around him. "Remember, I carried you around in my tummy for nine long months. We bonded before you even came into the world."

Aidan gifted her with a beatific smile.

"So maybe you can learn to love Daddy all over again. Right?" he asked with his head cocked. "Then we can be a real family."

"Um…well, it's possible, Aidan. But I don't want you to count on—" A knock on the door interrupted her.

The door opened and Liam peered in, his eyes full of questions. "How's it going in here?"

"What do you say? Did we get everything straightened out?" Ruby asked, leaning in to tickle him. Aidan burst into giggles and tried his best to fend her off.

"Better," Aidan said with a grin in his father's direction.

"Why don't you come out here and spend some time with your uncle before he takes off?" Liam asked. "He's meeting some friends in town."

"I still need to show him my fire truck," Aidan said, jumping up from his bed.

"And after your uncle leaves we're going to talk about throwing the fire truck," Liam said in a stern voice. "That was unacceptable."

"I'm sorry I did that," he said, his voice full of contrition. With a nod from his father, Aidan scooted out of the room.

As soon as they were alone, Ruby heaved a tremendous sigh. "I know you're probably wondering what happened. Long story short, Aidan overheard Kyle and I talking about us. He was pretty upset to hear I don't remember being in love with you."

Liam walked over and sat beside her on the bed. "He wants the fairy tale. With all the trimmings."

"And I burst his bubble. Great move on my part," Ruby said with a groan.

"I know this can't be easy for you."

"It's not. It's the worst feeling in the world to not be

able to remember who I am and the things I felt, the people I cared about, the very things that made me Ruby Prescott," she admitted, sniffing back tears. All of a sudden she felt like a stranger in a foreign land. Nothing made sense at the moment. Her brain felt fuzzy and her soul was weary.

Liam reached out and grazed his knuckles against Ruby's cheek. Instead of shying away from his touch, she felt comforted by it. "Please don't cry. That could bring me to my knees."

"I feel like I'm letting everyone down." Her voice trembled. Seeing Kyle and disappointing Aidan had cemented it. She was fumbling through town without a clue as to anything more than her name and a few remembrances…snippets in time that didn't amount to a hill of beans in the scheme of things. She couldn't access the memories that mattered most. Loving and being loved.

What is the point of even staying here in Love? As soon as that thought escaped, her son's innocent face flashed before her eyes.

"What? Disappointing us? That's not true," Liam said. "I realize you agreed to stay on here in town because of our son. I don't think I've expressed in words how grateful I am. You could have left on the next seaplane back to Denver. But you didn't. You had a little faith in me. I'm asking you now to have some in yourself."

"I suppose I'm feeling a bit sorry for myself at the moment. Everyone remembers me and, on some level, they expect me to have memories of them. But, for the most part, I don't. At the Moose Café I saw the sadness in Paige's eyes when she realized it wouldn't be wise to hug me. She remembers me as her dear friend, but that doesn't really mean anything to me. And she could see it! Same thing with Kyle. I could see the love shining in his eyes and I felt a connection, but I keep beating myself up for not feeling more motherly." She pressed her hands against her heart. "What if these memories never come back? Where does that leave me?"

"Give yourself a break, Ruby. You've barely been back in town for forty-eight hours. The memories might come back to you, but if they don't, you can still build bridges with the people in your life who care about you. Look at you and Aidan! He still thinks you're a rock star."

"I wish that I felt that way about myself," she said. "At the café earlier, my hands were shaking like a leaf."

"We all get scared sometimes," Liam said. "You should see me when I have a patient whose illness is challenging to diagnose."

"I must have been brave to be in the search-and-rescue profession." Ruby hadn't asked many questions about her previous line of work. She was really curious about it and what had led her down that road. Liam had told her that both her parents had died in a car accident. Perhaps that had motivated her to rescue others so their families wouldn't have to deal with the loss and heartache.

She wasn't sure if it was her imagination, but Liam seemed to stiffen at the mention of her job. Maybe it was a touchy subject due to the Colorado mission.

"You weren't afraid of anything. Not ever."

"So I was tough?" she asked.

"As nails," Liam said. "Nothing ever scared you... not wolves or bears or delivering Aidan without a single pain reliever. You've always been a mighty warrior."

"What about you? Were you afraid when I went out on a mission?"

"I was always afraid of losing you...your job scared me. Not that I wasn't proud of you, because I was awed and humbled by your service. But in my heart I was always dreading the day when I would get a call saying you'd been injured or worse."

"And worse happened, didn't it?" She couldn't imagine Liam having to deal with the terrible news from Colorado. His wife had gone to rescue people, only to perish in the process.

"It did. And the bottom fell out of my world."

Something glimmered in his eyes that hinted of deep pain and loss. This man had been through the ringer. She wished she could do something to take away everything he'd endured at the loss of her. But it wasn't possible. At the moment all she could do was pray. She prayed for Aidan. And Kyle. She also prayed for her and Liam, that somehow all would be revealed to them in the weeks and months to come. And that whatever decisions they came to about their marriage and her future here in Love, they would both be at peace with them.

Chapter Seven

Liam sat in the office of his clinic, waiting for his ten o'clock patient to arrive. As it usually did, his mind wandered to Ruby. For the past week he had been trying to figure out ways to help Ruby settle into her old life. At the moment he remained stumped. How could he help his wife find her way back?

The situation was weighing heavily on him. He hated to see Ruby suffer. It reminded him way too much of how unhappy she'd been in those dark days before she'd left them for that last rescue operation. There had been a lot of tears and arguments leading to the unraveling of their marriage.

Just thinking about it made his chest tighten and sweat gather on his forehead. Losing Ruby seemed to be a recurring theme in his life. He didn't know how he could stand to do it another time if her unhappiness caused her to leave town. It was the main reason he was holding back and trying not to invest too much emotionally in their relationship even though she had decided to stay in town for an indefinite period to see how things played out. What if she ultimately decided it was too difficult to remain in Love and headed back to Colorado? The truth was that Aidan wouldn't be the only one with a broken heart. His own would be shattered…and not for the first time.

After hearing the jingle of the bell on the front door, he cast a quick glance at his desk clock. His patient, Myrtle Maplethorpe, was early today. Liam wouldn't be surprised if she had arrived early to get the scoop about Ruby's return. He got up from his chair and walked into the reception area. Cameron was standing there with Emma cradled against his chest. She had her thumb firmly rooted in her mouth and her eyes were closed. His niece looked as sweet as ever. Wanda, his receptionist, was gazing at Emma with adoration.

"I was just about to buzz you, Doctor Prescott," Wanda said, her expression sheepish. She walked behind the front desk and sat down.

"Hey, Cam. What brings you over here?" Liam greeted his brother.

Cameron's features looked pinched. A frown marred his brow. "I think Emma might be sick. She's been fussing quite a bit. She wouldn't go down for her nap today and she feels a little warm."

"Does she have a temperature?"

"I'm not sure. I figured I would just bring her over here so you could check her out. Paige is at that meeting over in Homer today, representing Lovely Boots. Declan flew her over. I'm on Dad duty."

Lovely Boots was a corporation based in Love that

sold genuine Alaskan boots created by Hazel. A majority of the proceeds went toward the town of Love in the hopes of improving the local economy. "Let's go into one of the rooms so I can check her out," Liam said, ushering his brother down the hall.

Once they were inside, Liam reached out for Emma. At first she resisted, snuggling deeper into her father's chest. With all the gentleness in the world, Liam plucked her out of Cameron's arms and placed her on the examination table. Her eyes flew open and for a moment tears welled in her eyes. "It's okay, Emma. It's me. Uncle Liam." His voice was soft and tender.

Emma immediately turned and held her arms up toward Cameron. A small cry escaped her lips. "Shh, sweet baby girl. Uncle Liam needs to examine you so he can make you feel better."

He'd never quite seen such a tortured expression on Cameron's face. There was nothing like being a father to tie you up in knots.

"Why don't you hold her while I take her vitals?" Liam suggesting, realizing Cameron needed this for comfort as much as Emma did.

Relief washed over Cameron's face as he picked up Emma and rocked her in his arms.

For the next few minutes Liam examined his niece. "She has a temperature. It's 102."

"That's high," Cameron said, biting his lip. "Poor little thing. I knew something was off." He pressed a kiss against Emma's cheek.

The moment Liam checked in her ears he hit pay dirt. "She's got a double ear infection, Cam, which is no doubt making it difficult for her to lie down. It increases the pressure and pain in her ears. Has she had one before?"

Cameron shrugged. "Not that I know of. At least not in the last eight months or so."

Cameron's answer referenced the fact that he had only known his daughter Emma since Paige had brought her to Love eight months ago. For the first fourteen months of her life, Cameron hadn't known of Emma's existence. Upon her return to town, Cameron and Paige had quickly fallen back in love and gotten married. They were now happily raising their daughter together.

"She's going to need a course of antibiotics and some drops for the ear pain. We don't want this infection to get any worse."

"I'm glad I didn't wait to come in. This way Emma will be on the mend right away."

"I'll call the prescription in to the pharmacy. I think I have some drops here somewhere." Liam turned around and rummaged in his cabinets. "Here we are." He handed Cameron a vial of drops that would take away some of Emma's discomfort. He winked at his brother. "This way you and Paige might not have to stay up all night with a screaming child."

"Bless you. It sure comes in handy having a doctor for a brother," Cameron said with a grin.

"Glad to hear it," Liam said. It made him feel good inside to know that he'd made his brother's road a bit easier. It was worth all the years of struggle and schooling to be able to make his beautiful niece feel better. Being a doctor in his Alaskan hometown was extremely gratifying. He truly believed it was his calling and that God had led him on this path.

"I've been meaning to catch up with you," Cameron said. "I know you've been really busy the last few days."

"It's been a whirlwind, that's for sure."

"So, how does it feel to be reunited with Ruby? It's pretty incredible, huh?"

"I feel blessed."

"And? What else? I know Ruby has amnesia, but has it been romantic between the two of you? Moonlight and roses?"

"No, it hasn't," Liam said in a curt voice. "Ruby doesn't remember me. She has no inkling of what we were to one another. The love we shared. The ups and downs."

Cameron frowned. "Downs? You two were perfect together. Blissful."

"That's not true," Liam snapped. Cameron's eyes widened. "Sorry," he apologized. "I didn't mean to snap at you. Before Ruby went on that Colorado mission, the two of us were having problems. We couldn't agree on her job. I thought she was tempting fate by putting herself at risk on these various missions, and she had no intention of giving it up. We went round and round about it with no resolution."

"Seriously?" Cameron asked, appearing stunned. "I had no idea you were going through that. From the outside looking in, the two of you seemed so content." He ran his hands over Emma's hair. She had fallen asleep on his chest.

"I didn't tell anyone. I thought Ruby and I would work it out ourselves. Until the day she took off her wedding rings and asked for a legal separation. It was the day before she left us. We had been fighting non-stop… I guess she had reached her breaking point. Truthfully, so had I. But I never imagined us not being together. Until she threw it out there."

"Liam. You would have worked through it if—" Cameron's words dangled in the air.

"If Ruby hadn't been presumed dead on that Colorado mountain?" Liam scratched his chin. "I don't know. It broke my heart when she took off her rings. And even though I prayed we would find our way, we never got the opportunity."

"But you have it now, don't you?" Cameron asked. "She's back… God led her straight to Love and toward you and Aidan. That has to mean something."

Liam swallowed past the bile rising in his throat. "It's hard to put my heart on the line again, knowing that if she remembers the past she might toss me aside all over again. Maybe she really, truly, had fallen out of love with me. Perhaps that's why she hasn't had a single memory about me…and what we were to one another. And I'm starting to feel guilty about making her believe everything was peaches and cream between us, when that's far from the truth."

"Liam, you and Ruby were a love story. I can't believe you'd give up on that so easily. Most people don't get second chances at love."

"I'm not giving up. I just don't know how to protect my heart on this journey with Ruby. I want Aidan to have the thing he wants most in the world, but I also want my life back. The life I always imagined."

"Then go for it, bro. Don't let fear stop you." Cameron's voice was laced with encouragement.

Just then the clinic door jingled again, heralding the arrival of Myrtle Maplethorpe, aka the Duchess. Myrtle, the local historian, was also known as Love's resident town gossip. Liam could hear her high-pitched voice emanating from the other room as she greeted Wanda.

"I should get this little lady home and call Paige. It sounds like your next appointment is here."

They walked out into the waiting room together, both marveling at how soundly Emma was sleeping. The resiliency of children always amazed Liam, both personally and professionally.

Myrtle was standing there in front of the main desk, resplendent in aqua from head to toe. She peered at them through her Coke-bottle glasses.

"Well, hello, Dr. Liam. Cameron. Oh, and a darling little Prescott princess." Myrtle's tone trilled.

"She's a little under the weather with an ear infection," Cameron explained.

"Oh, those can be dreadful," Myrtle said. "I hope the wee one feels better."

"Thanks. Nice to see you, Myrtle." Cameron adjusted Emma on his chest. "See you later, Liam. And thanks for everything. If you need to talk, you know where to find me."

As Liam turned back to Myrtle, she narrowed her eyes at him. "Sounds like you've been leaning on your brother for advice. I've been called a good listener a time or two," she said. "If you need a listening ear."

Liam almost burst out laughing. Myrtle was notorious for spreading people's private business all around town. There was no way he was going to confide in her all his doubts and fears about Ruby. If he did, it would spread all over town like wildfire. Myrtle wasn't a bad person, but she certainly wasn't someone he could trust with his personal business.

"That's very kind of you to offer. Why don't we go check out your heartburn?"

As he led Myrtle into one of the examining rooms, he found himself wishing his issues with Ruby were as easy to solve as a simple case of heartburn.

Ruby felt a little bit nervous about showing up at Liam's clinic unannounced, but after consulting with Aidan, they had decided that surprising him with lunch was a brilliant idea. She needed to step out a little bit on faith and embrace the life she'd once made for herself. On some level she had to accept that the woman she'd once been had chosen this life for herself. She had picked Liam. Although she'd made strides with Aidan, she had deliberately been distant from Liam. Knowing they had been a storybook couple felt intimidating. Out of her reach.

How could she ever live up to the fairy tale of her and Liam? But was it right to not even try to forge something with her husband? She had once vowed to love this man for a lifetime. And with every day she spent here in Love, she was seeing the truth about this man with her own eyes. He was a loving father. Generous. And attentive. The fact that he could have been Mr. Alaska sure didn't hurt. He was the most eye-catching man she had ever known.

She had forced herself to take a good look in the mirror to examine her truths. Then she'd had a long talk with God. He had helped her see things more clearly. It was easier to have one foot in Love rather than invest everything in a life she couldn't quite grasp. That meant she had an escape hatch. If she wasn't fully invested, she could always head back to Denver. In the back of her mind, that's what she had been doing ever since she arrived in town. And even though she had agreed to stay on for a bit, there was no commitment to relocate to Love. Her hands weren't tied. But it also meant that she wasn't giving fully of herself. That had to change!

Now, armed with a fully loaded picnic basket, she was venturing out on a limb and seeing what came of it. And her pint-size companion seemed as excited about this outing as a kid on Christmas morning. He'd been the one to show her where to find the keys to the spare car sitting in the garage. Thankfully, due to Colorado's climate, Ruby was used to driving on snow-packed roads. She took her time and handled the unfamiliar roads like a pro.

Liam's clinic was situated in a small, white clapboard house at the end of Jarvis Street. A sweet sign welcomed them to Dr. Prescott's Office. A festive Christmas wreath hung on the door, adorned with bright red ribbons and candy canes. Adorable snowmen clung to the windows. Ruby couldn't imagine a more cheery-looking doctor's office.

As they walked through the front door, silver bells

jangled from above them. Aidan giggled and pointed. He began swinging the door back and forth so the bells continued to chime. Ruby shook her head and laughed. The sound of footsteps alerted them to Liam's arrival before he came around the corner. The look of joyful surprise etched on his face was priceless. Warmth settled in Ruby's chest at the sight of him. All her nerves immediately settled.

"Hey! I didn't expect to see the two of you. I thought it might be Wanda coming back from her lunch break."

"We're taking you to lunch, Daddy." Aidan pointed at the picnic basket. "And you won't even have to leave your office."

Ruby held up the basket. "We hope you haven't eaten yet. A little birdie told me you usually eat around this time, so we decided to bring lunch to you."

Liam's face lit up like a Christmas tree. He grinned from ear to ear. "Thank you for thinking of me. It's always nice to break up the day like this." He motioned them down the hall. "Let's go set up in one of the empty offices. I have about forty-five minutes until my next patient."

Ruby trailed after Liam and Aidan. Once they were in the office she pulled a red tablecloth from inside her shoulder bag and began spreading it out on the small table.

"We brought chicken sandwiches and potato salad and cupcakes. Plus, a bag of my favorite chips." Aidan rattled off the menu. "And a bottle of sparkling cider."

"Cupcakes! Wow," Liam said. "You're going to spoil me."

"We did a little baking this morning," Ruby said.

"For some reason I really enjoy making cupcakes." Ruby had discovered when she was living with Trudy and Ezra that baking was her forte. It had kept her busy in the weeks and months during her recovery. And the older couple had appreciated having someone help them around the house.

"You were always an excellent cook, Ruby," Liam said. "Your specialty was reindeer pizza."

Ruby turned toward him. "Reindeer pizza? Seriously?"

"It was your favorite." Liam rubbed his stomach. "Not only to eat, but you baked it to sheer perfection." Liam kissed his fingers and lifted them in the air. Ruby chuckled at the gesture.

Ruby began taking the plates and utensils out of the basket. She lifted the sandwiches out and placed one on each plate, along with a dollop of potato salad. Aidan and Liam sat at the table.

Ruby made a face. "No offense, but I can't imagine being partial to reindeer anything."

Liam shot her a knowing smile. "Don't knock it until you try it."

"Don't hold your breath," Ruby said in a singsong voice.

"Hey! Wanna see how long I can hold my breath?" Aidan asked. He puffed out his cheeks.

"After lunch you can impress us, A-man. Let's just focus on this wonderful meal for the moment."

"Let's pray over the food," Aidan said. He reached out his hands on either side of him. Both Liam and Ruby linked their hands with his.

"May I?" Ruby asked. Liam nodded.

"Go for it," Aidan said. His encouragement made Ruby grin. He was such a joyful child. It spoke well of the way Aidan had raised him in the aftermath of the tragedy. There wasn't a single thing about her son that she didn't love to pieces. Although the idea of caring so much about him scared her a little bit, she was enjoying her role as his mother.

She was acting on instinct and trying to listen to him and gauge his needs. *Fake it until you make it.* The expression popped into her mind. Ruby didn't have all the answers, but she was determined to try to be the best mother possible.

She bowed her head. "Thank You for this food, Lord, and for the blessings You continue to bestow on us. Thank You for this day and for all the ones to follow."

"Amen," Liam and Aidan said in unison.

They began to eat their lunch, enjoying a companionable silence as they devoured the chicken sandwiches.

This was nice, Ruby thought. For once her mind wasn't whirling with doubts.

"So, how is your day going, Dad?" Aidan asked, sounding older than his years.

Liam grinned. "Pretty interesting. A very familiar face popped by."

"Jasper!" Aidan guessed. "Was it his heart again?" he asked, referencing the heart problems that had sidelined Jasper almost two years ago.

"Nope. It was your cousin, Emma. She had an ear infection."

"Oh, that's yucky!" Aidan made a face. "I'm going to say a prayer for her tonight before I go to sleep."

"Praying for her is a wonderful idea," Liam said. He reached out and patted Aidan on the shoulder. Father and son. When they were sitting next to each other like this, Ruby could see the resemblance. They had the same dark brown hair and their facial expressions were identical. Aidan had her eyes, though—they were a warm shade of brown.

"Someone slipped this under the door this morning after you left." Ruby slid a brightly colored card across the table. Liam wiped his hands on his napkin then picked up the card and read it out loud. "'You are invited to a Get To Know Us tea party. Get dressed up and come spend some time with us. Tea will be served promptly at four o'clock at Hazel's Lodge.'" There were names scrawled across the bottom. Hazel. Grace. Paige. Sophie. Honor. And Annie.

Ruby had almost burst into tears the moment she'd read the gorgeous invitation. These ladies were being thoughtful and caring. They were trying to be sensitive of the fact that she had amnesia and didn't have memories to draw on. And they were pulling her into the fold by extending this thoughtful invitation to her. Although she had acquaintances in Colorado, her closest friends had been Ezra and Trudy, who were senior citizens. Ruby loved them dearly, but there hadn't been any real common ground.

In Love, Alaska, she had blood relations and family ties. A best friend. A hunky husband who made her stomach do flip-flops. Whether she remembered it or not, she had history.

"So…are you going?" Liam asked. He was tapping his fingers on the table as if her answer was important to him.

"Of course. How could I say no?" Ruby asked. "It will give me an opportunity to renew some friendships and step out on that limb. Not to mention it will give me a reason to get a little gussied up. I'm getting tired of wearing nothing but jeans and leggings." She felt a little self-conscious as Liam's eyes honed in on her like laser beams.

"I think you look pretty awesome in jeans," Liam said, flashing her a cheeky grin.

She raised her hands to her heated cheeks. The compliment washed over her like warm rain. As if he needed to do anything else to make her heart go pitter-patter. During lunch she had struggled to tear her eyes away from his jaw-droppingly handsome face. Several times her gaze had lingered way too long. She'd been certain he had noticed her perusal, although he hadn't let on.

What had it been like, she wondered, to be this man's wife? To be adored and protected by such a strong, upstanding man must have been amazing. Liam was a hottie. It was undeniable. In his white lab coat and with his stethoscope hanging around his neck, he looked even more impressive.

But allowing her mind to veer toward romance wasn't smart. Not when she still didn't have any recollection of him or their life together. How could she allow herself to fall for Liam when she didn't know who she herself was?

"Well, we should get going and let you get back to work," Ruby said in a brisk voice. She stood and smoothed her hands against the fabric of her jeans. She began tidying the table and packing up the remnants from lunch.

"Aw. Is it time to leave already?" Aidan pouted.

Liam stood and lifted Aidan into his arms. "No worries, A-man. I'll be home before you know it. Maybe we can take a walk in the woods behind the house and leave some food for your reindeers."

"Yes!" Aidan cried as he raised his fist in the air.

Liam always knew what to say to make things better for their son. He did it so effortlessly, she couldn't help but feel a twinge of envy. Had she once had that particular talent? A memory tugged at her. She was pushing Aidan in a little swing to stop him from crying. Every time he went up in the air he pumped his little legs. For a moment she simply reveled in the recollection. It was real! She just knew it. And before long she would be remembering other things—perhaps about her friendship with Paige, her parents, Aidan's first moments… and her romantic journey with Liam.

Please, Lord, let me remember more about my life in Love. I don't want to walk around not feeling whole anymore. Let me learn more about myself so I can be a better woman. Not just for myself, but for Aidan and Liam, as well.

Chapter Eight

Ever since Ruby's return, coming home after work had been the highlight of Liam's day. As he drove down the private lane leading to the house, his chest always felt as if it might burst with expectation. It was a strange feeling since it reminded him of the early days when he'd first fallen in love with Ruby. Back then he had been full of a mixture of excitement and dread. He had been so afraid of losing her. It had always seemed to Liam that being with Ruby was like catching lightning in a bottle. It still stunned him to this day that all of his prayers had been answered when she'd fallen deeply in love with him.

God had blessed them both. And even though the current situation wasn't ideal, he had to remind himself to stay focused on the blessings.

Liam drove into the driveway and stared at the log cabin nestled in the woods. A soft, amber-colored light emanated from inside. This was his haven. He had always loved their abode, but now it felt like home again.

During Ruby's absence he had tried to fill the house with as much love as he could, but he'd never been able to replicate all of the things Ruby had infused into their home. A woman's touch. A mother's nurturing instincts. A soft place to fall.

And despite her amnesia, she still brought her own ray of light along with her. It had subtly transformed their house into a home.

With each and every day that passed, he was finding it hard to imagine being without Ruby ever again. Although the question still remained. Would Ruby stay on in Love? Or would she return to the life she'd been living in Denver? The very thought of her leaving made his chest tighten with sorrow.

A flash of color caught his eye just as he was about to mount the stairs leading to the porch. A slight figure—bigger than Aidan—stood right on the edge of the area leading toward the forest.

The illumination from the porch shed a little light on the shadowy figure. It was Ruby. Placing his briefcase on the steps, he turned around and began walking in her direction.

The crunching sound of his footsteps on the snow-packed ground filled the silence with every step he took. Ruby swung her eyes toward him as he approached. With her red coat and white, tasseled hat and matching mittens, she looked utterly charming.

"Hi, Liam."

"Hey, Ruby. What's going on out here? It's pretty cold to be outside now that the temperatures have dropped."

She waved her mittened hand toward the woods. "I

heard something out there. It sounded like an animal crying out. Aidan is watching television, so I figured I'd check things out." She shrugged. A sheepish expression crept over her face. "I thought maybe I could save whatever creature was out here raising a ruckus."

Liam cast his eyes toward the woods. "It was most likely a bird of some variety. A loon or owl. Or a beaver perhaps."

She bit her lip. "It was such a plaintive cry. Heartbreaking really. It stopped right before you drove up."

"You don't want to venture out in the woods at night, Ruby. I should have remembered to tell you that. It's fairly common to come up against wolves or even bears in these parts." He felt like kicking himself for failing to warn his wife about the potential dangers in Alaska. It was still hard to wrap his head around all of the things she no longer remembered.

Her eyes widened. "Yikes. So most likely a wolf was hunting its prey."

He smiled at her. "Most likely. They've been known to go after moose and caribou, as well."

Ruby nodded. "And they've gone after humans, too, which makes it foolish for me to have come out here to investigate." Her expression radiated frustration.

"Not foolish," he corrected. "Caring about animals is compassionate. Part of living in Alaska means being aware of the risks, however small they might be."

She huffed out a small breath. "It's strange to not remember such vital things." Ruby ducked her head. He could see her lip trembling.

He reached out and tipped her chin up, acting on impulse. "I know this whole experience must be scary for you. I can't imagine how difficult it must be to not remember so many things. For what it's worth, I think you're a brave woman, Ruby Prescott. You always have been."

They locked gazes. Her warm brown eyes flared with uncertainty. "That's the thing, though. I don't feel courageous. You told me earlier that I was a brave person, but maybe that was the old Ruby. Most days I feel like I'm stumbling around in the dark without a flashlight. I wish I could remember Aidan's favorite foods and the things that scare him."

"It's understandable that you feel that way. When I first opened my clinic here in Love, I had a lot of people questioning me." He let out a throaty laugh. "There were residents who still viewed me as a kid, even though I was a fully grown adult who was a medical doctor. It got to me. Pretty soon I was doubting my own qualifications and skills. I wondered if I'd bitten off more than I could chew."

Ruby's eyes blinked furiously as she looked at him. A fragile hope glistened in her eyes. Ruby wanted so badly to get her memories back. It shimmered from deep inside her like a beacon.

Liam ached for her. Had he been so worried about Aidan's feelings that he'd minimized how difficult this whole process must be for Ruby? Was he guilty of being selfish?

"And obviously you worked through it, right?" she asked, drawing him out of his thoughts.

"I did. Time worked wonders on my self-confidence.

And with every day I became a little braver, just like you are."

"I'm trying to be patient, but sometimes I just wish all my memories would come flooding back to me. There are so many questions rattling around in my brain. I'm excited about the tea party invitation, but I'm also fretting about it. What if I don't know what to say to them?"

"I know you're still getting back fragments of your memory, so you don't remember them just yet. But those ladies love you. Honor. Hazel. Paige. They'd walk through fire for you."

Tears welled in Ruby's eyes. "It humbles me to hear that."

"And don't worry about not knowing what to say. There's a saying that true friends know the song in your heart and can repeat it back to you if you've forgotten the words. That's the type of friends you have in your corner."

"That's a beautiful sentiment," Ruby said with a nod, the corners of her mouth lifting ever so slightly in a smile. She wiped her hand across her brow. "Phew. I guess that means I was a pretty decent human being," she quipped. "If I had been a total nightmare, I wouldn't have such amazing friends."

"You've always led with your heart," he said in a low voice. "And your kindness and loyalty to everyone in your circle never wavered."

Liam looked down at her, admiring the stunning beauty of his remarkable wife. He knew he was staring at her, but he couldn't help it. It might take him the rest of his life to get his fill of her after being under the belief that she was gone forever.

"Maybe we should go back inside," Ruby said, looking toward the house. "I'm sure Aidan is wondering where I am."

Liam chuckled. He could just imagine Aidan transfixed by his favorite science-fiction television show. "He's probably still glued to the screen."

Ruby giggled, showcasing the sweet sound of her laughter. "I have noticed that he can't be disturbed at this time of night. He really loves all the space travel and extraterrestrials."

He felt a surge of emotion rise inside him. This was pure Ruby. The infectious joy. Her utter radiance. The desire to protect a defenseless animal. It was all the best things about the woman he'd married. Bit by bit, she was coming back to him.

At this very moment he wanted to kiss her more than he'd ever wanted anything else in his life. And the way she was looking at him, with her face turned upward and her brown eyes brimming with emotion, made him think she wanted to be kissed.

Liam took a step closer. He reached out and placed his hands on either side of her face. "Ruby," he murmured, lowering his head toward her. He watched as she closed her eyes in expectation of the kiss. Her long, black lashes fluttered. He though he heard her let out a sigh.

"Hey! What's taking so long?" The high-pitched child's voice came out of nowhere.

"Aidan," Ruby said, her eyes blinking open. She turned

toward the house where their son stood in the doorway, looking in their direction.

"Hey, Aidan. We were just checking on something," Liam called out. "We'll be right there."

"When's dinner?" Aidan shouted. "I'm as hungry as a bear."

Liam let out a groan. There was no way he was going to try to kiss Ruby with Aidan screaming in the background. Besides, their son had ruined the perfect moment for their kiss. He loved Aidan dearly, but his timing was horrendous.

"I have a casserole in the oven," Ruby said. "I need to take it out before it overcooks."

Liam simply nodded. He felt a stab of disappointment so sharp it made his ribs ache. Why did this feel like such a setback? He knew his feelings were tied up in wanting things to get back to normal and his fears that Ruby might not stick around Love long enough for them to work on their future. In this instance, a kiss would have allowed him to take a giant leap forward in their relationship. It would have given him hope. As it was, he felt as if he was continually walking on eggshells.

As they made their way, side by side, toward the house, Liam felt a tugging on his heartstrings as he enjoyed the steady presence by his side.

Thank You, Lord, for giving me another shot at getting things right in my marriage. I promise to be a little more patient and to learn from the mistakes I made in the past. I won't squander this opportunity.

There would be other moments for him and Ruby.

He just needed to be patient and to appreciate the simple blessings.

Aidan was waiting for them at the door. Never in a million years had he believed his son would have the opportunity to spend time with his mother again and that the three of them would be able to live as a family.

God's grace was a mighty thing indeed.

"I'm so grateful for GPS," Ruby said as she navigated the winding back roads that led to Hazel's residence. She was driving Liam's truck rather than the spare car. Liam had told her that he felt better about her driving a truck with all-wheel drive and studded tires than a car that had been sitting in the garage for eons. If she hadn't been focusing so intently on the road, she might have been able to admire the stunning vista stretched out in front of her. Love, Alaska, was a picturesque fishing village straight out of a postcard.

Thankfully, between Liam and the Moose Crossing signs, she had been made acutely aware of the moose population in town. When three moose slowly made their way across the road, Ruby almost had to pick her jaw up off the floorboard. There was something majestic and beautiful about those humongous animals roaming freely about the land. But she also knew how dangerous they could be. As soon as they had crossed over, Ruby continued down the road. She sucked in a deep breath at the sight of large mountains looming in the distance. The raw beauty here in Alaska was unparalleled.

She let out a cry of triumph when she saw a wooden sign announcing the Black Bear Cabins. As she wound her way up the hill and drove past reddish-brown cabins, another sign with an arrow pointed the way toward the lodge.

As soon as Ruby rang the bell, the door swung open. Hazel was standing there, a welcoming smile on her face. She was wearing a bright pink sweater with a skirt that went all the way down to her ankles. Feeling a bit nervous, Ruby stuck out the bouquet of flowers she had brought as a hostess gift. "They're lovely," Hazel raved. "How did you know I loved forget-me-nots? Come on in."

"Thank you," she said as she entered Hazel's home. "Aidan helped me pick them out. And he told me that forget-me-nots are the official state flower, so that seemed perfect."

The moment Ruby entered Hazel's abode she felt as if she had been transported into a vintage era. There were so many elegant touches. Gleaming hardwood floors. Stained-glass windows. A grand spiral staircase. "Everyone is already in the parlor, so follow me," Hazel instructed with a wave of her hand.

Once they stepped inside, Ruby was greeted with a vibrant chorus of hellos. All the women had dressed up for the occasion. In addition to Hazel, she knew two of the women—Paige and Honor.

"I'm Sophie Miller." A stunning woman with fiery red hair and an infectious grin held out her hand to her. "Nice to meet you, Ruby."

"I'm Annie O'Rourke." Annie stepped forward and treated her to a warm smile. With her peaches-and-cream complexion and dark brown hair, she exuded sweetness. Her vintage emerald-colored cocktail dress was magnificent.

Hazel rubbed her hands together. "Well, we're just waiting for Grace to get here. Ruby, we wanted to host this tea party so you could see that you've got friends here in Love," Hazel explained. "And to extend you a hearty welcome back to the town that adores you."

"Everything is lovely," Ruby said as her glance swept across the table. It had been set with beautiful blue-and-white china. In front of every place setting sat a peacock feather.

"I'm getting pretty good at hosting these shindigs," Hazel boasted.

"You're a real pro," Sophie declared, gushing, her Southern accent on full display.

"One of these days we're going to host a party in your honor," Annie said, patting Hazel on her shoulder.

Hazel scrunched up her face. "Well, I'm overdue for a bridal shower," she grumbled. "Jasper has had me waiting so long for a proposal."

The parlor door opened. Grace was standing in the doorway with Boone right behind her, dwarfing his wife with his height. "Sorry I'm late, but I had a few technical difficulties."

Honor quickly reached her sister-in-law's side. "Is everything okay?"

Boone's eyes twinkled with merriment. His smile couldn't have been wider. For the first time Ruby noticed the resemblance between the three brothers. Liam was a bit more reserved, but he was the most devastatingly handsome of the trio. Her female appreciation of her husband made her cheeks warm.

"My wife's stomach made getting behind the wheel very tricky. I've never seen anything like it," Boone chuckled. "Her belly was actually touching the steering wheel."

Grace playfully jabbed him in the side. "You're enjoying this way too much, sheriff."

He leaned down and pressed a tender kiss on Grace's lips. "Give me a call when you're winding things up here and I'll swing back by and pick you up." He tipped his sheriff's hat in their direction. "Nice to see you, ladies. Enjoy your tea party."

As soon as Boone left, the room erupted into sighs of appreciation.

"Grace, if you weren't my best friend I'd be jealous of that dreamy husband of yours. And that goes for you too, Ruby and Annie. I don't know what's wrong with me." Sophie flung her hands in the air. "I came to this town as part of Operation Love, but I still haven't found anyone who inspires me for anything greater than friendship."

"Don't fret about that, Sophie," Honor said in a gentle voice. "You'll find him. They say you find someone when you're not looking."

"Well, that rules me out," she joked, "since I've been looking since the day I arrived in town."

All the ladies laughed at Sophie's animated expression.

"Why don't we sit down and start the festivities?" Hazel suggested. Everyone began moving toward the table. "Just sit anywhere. There's no assigned seating."

Ruby ended up next to Paige and Honor. There was quite a spread laid out for them. Gleaming silver dishes held cucumber sandwiches, lemon tarts, pastry puffs filled with lobster, scones with blueberry compote, mini pumpkin muffins and bagels with salmon spread. Ruby felt her tummy grumble in appreciation of the vast array of treats.

"Annie, could you serve the tea?" Hazel asked. "I'm Miss Butterfingers. I don't want to send anyone to Liam's clinic with hot tea burns. Jasper would never let me live that one down."

As Annie walked around the table and filled everyone's teacup, conversation began to flow as the ladies settled in and helped themselves to the food.

Grace spoke directly to Ruby from across the table. "I just want you to know, Ruby, that I haven't lived in Love very long myself. I came here as a journalist and ended up falling in love with Boone in rather quick fashion. When I first arrived here, I felt like I'd landed on a different planet. This must be very overwhelming to you. Although my circumstances were different, I can relate a little bit to how it must feel."

"I can also testify to how it feels to be a newcomer to Love," Sophie added, helping herself to another muffin. "Back in Saskell, Georgia, where I'm from, we hadn't seen snow since I was a little tyke no more than Aidan's age. So the climate here has been a little bit challenging. That was a shocker, along with getting used to the hours of sunlight depending on the time of year." She shook her head. "And I still can't wrap my head around all the single men roaming around this town."

"Add me to that list," Annie said as she placed the teapot back on the table and sat. "I came to Love to be town librarian and as part of Jasper's Operation Love campaign." She let out a sigh that sounded a lot like contentment. "I think my adjustment was easier because I was really looking to be part of a community. With no family to speak of, I found my haven here in Love."

"Sounds like you all did," Ruby said, moved by the fact that all three women had found their destinies in this quaint town. "It does feel like a whole new world sometimes. It's not the Alaskan lifestyle or the climate…at least not yet. What's bugging me is that I still can't access most of my memories." She let out a huff of frustration. "I have to accept the fact that I might never be able to recover the bulk of my past."

"Ask for God's grace in helping you face that possibility. If you lean on Him, He'll see you through this." Paige's words were heartfelt and wise.

Ruby had been leaning on God, but she needed to speak to Him about her fears and the things that were holding her back. And perhaps she needed to open up to Liam, as well.

"Why don't you and Paige go sit down and talk while we clean up?" Hazel suggested. "And, Grace, go sit on the settee. It makes me uncomfortable seeing you stand on your feet for long stretches of time. Your feet will get swollen."

"You don't have to tell me twice," Grace teased as she struggled to get up from her seat. Honor gave her a slight push until she was standing upright. She placed her hand on her belly and ambled off to the living room.

All the other ladies headed to the kitchen, their arms filled with dishes to be washed.

"So, how are you settling in?" Paige reached out for Ruby's hand and squeezed it. The gesture felt like encouragement. Ruby hesitated for a moment. Paige was her sister-in-law, married to Liam's brother. She didn't want to say anything that could travel through the family grapevine.

"You don't need to worry about me passing any information along. We always had a pact that our conversations remained private." A gentle smile lit Paige's face. "That hasn't changed."

Ruby let out a sigh of relief. So far there really hadn't been anyone in Love that she could confide in. There was something calm and reassuring about Paige. She sent out very positive vibes. Ruby felt she could trust her.

"It's been a whirlwind, for lack of a better word. I'm sure it won't surprise you to hear that Liam has been patient and kind. I feel badly, though, because I keep seeing him look at me as if he's searching for his wife. But all he finds is me—a shell of my former self." She let out a little sob, shocked at the intensity of her own words.

"Oh, honey," Paige said in a comforting voice, "that must be so difficult…to feel as if you're disappointing him."

"That's exactly how I feel," she admitted, wiping away the tears from her face. "And I'm constantly wondering if I'm living up to the old Ruby as far as being a mother to Aidan. So far no one has given me a road map to follow."

"You have to remember, Ruby, that you aren't responsible for your amnesia. You were the victim of an accident. You lost two years of your life with your family. You're allowed to hurt and grieve and vent. And maybe you should express these feelings to Liam. I'm sure he's navigating through his own feelings of loss and confusion and pain."

Ruby allowed herself to cry. She'd been holding back for entirely too long. She felt Paige's comforting arm resting around her shoulder.

You never walk alone. She remembered Kyle saying that to her after the death of their parents. She would use her brother's advice now to guide her on her journey. Living in Colorado had been lonely at times. Her heart had yearned for connections. And now, sitting right beside her, was a dear friend who loved and supported her. She couldn't overlook that blessing.

"Thanks for saying that. I suppose I do feel guilty. My profession involved great risks to my personal safety. I can't help but feel that I caused my family a world of pain, and I'm still trying to connect to them in meaningful ways."

"Well, you need to know that in addition to being a first-class mother and a loving wife, you were amazing in your chosen field. You loved helping people and saving lives. You always said it made you feel ten feet tall to give them a shot at living another day."

Ruby found the topic of her profession fascinating. In the quiet hours between dark and dawn she had remained awake thinking about the fast-paced world of search and rescue. There were still so many questions she didn't know the answers to about her career. And she must have loved it immensely to risk life and limb on a regular basis.

"Do you know why I went into search and rescue?" She had a hunch it was tied up in the tragic loss of her parents, but she hadn't yet asked Liam.

"Yes. It was because of your parents. They died in a pretty horrific pile-up on a highway in Anchorage. Because of a delay in getting rescue workers to the scene, eight people died. There was a big outcry afterward in the media about it. Unfortunately, that was something we had in common. My mother also died in a car crash."

"So it bonded us?"

Paige grinned. "That, among other things. We were both in love with Prescott men, so that really jump-started our friendship."

"And we had to deal with Jasper," Ruby quipped.

Paige nodded enthusiastically. "Dealing with Jasper's antics and his constant comments about settling down with his grandsons bonded us for life. Now that I think of it, we should get medals of valor."

They shared a look that resulted in the two of them launching into fits of laughter.

Liam sat at the kitchen table filling out some paperwork. He'd closed the clinic early today so he could work from home this afternoon. Aidan was at a friend's house for a play date until suppertime. Ruby had gone to the tea party at Hazel's lodge, looking more gorgeous than ever. Without Ruby and Aidan puttering around, the house had a quiet, unnatural vibe to it.

How long did tea parties last, anyway? He missed his

wife. And he had nearly passed out at the sight of her in her tea party finery. His breathing had definitely gotten shaky. Her long hair had hung loose in soft waves. Other than a slash of red lining her lips, her face had been devoid of makeup. Ruby had dressed to the nines in a red, knee-length, cocktail dress with black lace at the hemline. She'd found the dress at the back of the closet they had once shared. Try as he might, he hadn't been able to dispose of Ruby's things. His family had said he was holding on to his grief, but now he had to wonder if God had been telling him to hold on and not let go.

Ruby was a beautiful woman. It had taken every ounce of his self-control not to sweep her up in his arms and kiss her senseless. He frowned. What made him think she would want that type of intimacy with him? Even though she was starting to remember little nuggets about him, it still didn't mean they were going to ride off into the sunset together. There was still a chasm of unresolved issues standing between them, and those issues would come to light if Ruby's memories returned. They still had mountains to climb before they could ever hope to get back what they'd lost.

A loud knocking interrupted his thoughts. Someone was at the front door. Maybe Ruby had forgotten her house key. He pushed up from his chair and strode to the front door, pulling it open in one fluid motion. Instead of his wife standing there, he found himself staring into the bluest pair of eyes he'd ever known. A pair almost identical to his own.

"Pop!" He almost did a double take. His father, Gareth Prescott, was standing on his doorstep. Tall, leanly muscled and good-looking, his father cut an impressive figure. His tanned features hinted at a lifestyle inconsistent with Alaska.

"Hey, Liam. Aren't you going to invite me in?" He slapped him on the shoulder as he walked past him and into the house. "It's been a while."

Liam almost couldn't believe his eyes. Wasn't his father somewhere in South America helping with a search-and-rescue mission? Not that he had the up-to-date information regarding his whereabouts. His father had always been a rolling stone, living his life on his own terms without any apologies to his kids. After his parents had divorced and gone their separate ways, both had left Alaska for warmer climates. Gareth's profession as a search-and-rescue leader had placed him on several operations with Ruby over the years. Liam hadn't seen his father since Ruby's memorial service. Although he had called a few times, Gareth's contact with his family had been limited.

Liam closed the front door and trailed after his father, who was walking toward the kitchen. "So, kiddo. How's Ruby doing? Jasper called me about her return. I couldn't believe it when he told me she had resurfaced with amnesia."

Liam put a lid on his annoyance as his father opened up the fridge and began poking around inside. "What Jasper said is the truth. She has flashes of memory, but for the most part she's a clean slate. It's been improving, though, since she's been back in Love. So there's hope."

His father poured himself a tall glass of lemonade. He took a lengthy sip. "That's a tough break, Liam."

"So what brings you back to Love? It's been a while," Liam said. Every instinct was telling him his father wasn't just here to check in on his family. The past had shown him that Gareth Prescott was most comfortable at a distance.

"Well, to be honest, I've been asked by the higher-ups to find out if Ruby is interested in coming back to work. They flew me out here to talk to her, find out if she's interested, or if she's even capable of doing so, what with her memory loss and all."

Anger—hot and fiery—pulsed through his veins. Search and rescue had already taken enough from them. It wasn't getting Ruby back. Not if he had anything to say about it.

All this time he had been agonizing about the past coming back to bite him. How wrong he had been. He hadn't seen this coming. Not by a long shot.

Liam let out a harsh laugh. "I should have known. You would never come back simply to check in on your kids or Aidan or to meet your newest grandchild, Emma. It's all about the work, right, Pop?"

His father held up his hands. "Liam, don't take this so personally."

"Save it. I don't want to hear it. And I don't want you coming around buzzing in Ruby's ear about how wonderful search-and-rescue missions are."

"I'm not looking to make any trouble," Gareth insisted. "We worked together. I wanted to see how she's doing. After all, she did suffer her injuries in the line of duty."

Liam took a steadying breath. What was it about his

father that always pushed all of his buttons? He wasn't sure how to put into words how nervy it was for him to show up here. This was one big slap in the face after a lifetime of disappointments. Where had he been for the last two years when Liam had been mired in grief?

"Ruby is fine. I'll make sure of it." He spit the words out.

"She has to make her own decisions, Liam," Gareth said in a softer tone. "Despite everything that's happened, she's a big girl."

"How many ways can I say this? Ruby's career in search and rescue is over. She nearly lost her life due to that profession. There's no way I'm ever going to allow her to go back. Not on my watch!"

"Liam!" Ruby's voice crashed over him like a bucket of ice water. He turned toward the doorway.

Ruby was standing there, a look of horror etched on her face. Her eyes wide, she was looking back and forth between him and his father.

"I could hear the two of you shouting from outside on the porch. What in the world is going on here?"

Ruby felt as if she had just walked into a war zone. Liam—calm, cool Liam—looked wild-eyed and fierce. He practically had steam coming out of his ears. And the gentleman he was speaking to seemed just as agitated. His brow furrowed, he looked like a kettle about to boil.

"Liam?" she repeated in a tentative voice. "What's going on?" The tension hanging in the air was palpable.

He shoved his hand through his hair then jerked his chin in the man's direction. "This is my father. He was just leaving." Liam's voice was curt, bordering on rude.

Ruby frowned. Liam hadn't mentioned anything at all about his father to her, other than the fact that he'd been on her search-and-rescue mission two years ago. Clearly, there had been a reason for that omission. Their relationship seemed frosty at best.

Liam's father stepped toward her. "Since Liam doesn't seem inclined to introduce us, I'll do the honors myself. I'm Gareth Prescott. I can tell by the look on your face that you don't remember me, but we were friends."

"You were there that day on the mountain," she said. She practically had to push the words out of her mouth. It felt like there were cotton balls lodged in her throat. Every time she thought about the accident, dread rose inside her.

There was something about seeing Liam's father that made her want to ask him a hundred questions about that terrible day. What had he seen? Had she really saved lives on the mountain? Perhaps by finding out the answers to her questions, the fear bottled up inside her might dissipate.

He darted a glance in Liam's direction. Liam glared at him. Gareth turned back to her. "I was there that day." He shook his head. "I wish I could have done something more for you. One minute you were standing there and the next thing we knew the snow-slip swallowed you up."

"You saw it?" Ruby asked.

"Yes, with my own eyes." He shuddered. "I never want to see anything like it ever again, although in the search-and-rescue business that's unlikely."

Something had been bothering Ruby. It was a tidbit

of a detail. She wasn't sure it was from that mission, but she had to ask Gareth.

"Was there a search-and-rescue dog there that day? A German shepherd."

"Ruby, why do you want to dredge this all up?" Liam asked. He had a tense expression on his face.

"Because it's part of me. That day changed my life. I don't know why, but talking about it helps."

"It just drags you back into the past," Liam said with a shake of his head.

"And it might help me trigger some more memories." She turned to Gareth. "Was there a rescue dog?"

"Yes," Gareth answered. "There was a dog there that day. He didn't make it."

"Rufus," she whispered. Images of a sweet, brown-and-black German shepherd flickered in her mind like snapshots. Her mouth went dry. "Did I—?"

"You trained him, Ruby. He was yours," Liam said, his voice suddenly tender.

Ruby wrapped her arms around her middle. The memories flashing before her eyes were poignant and powerful. Rufus as a puppy trailing after her in the snowy yard. Aidan playing with him. Liam taking him for walks. Ruby training him as a certified search-and-rescue dog.

And he had died on that mountain in her arms.

She heard Liam's voice through a fog. He was telling his father it was time for him to leave. Out of nowhere it felt like she couldn't breathe. She began to breathe rapidly, her chest rising and falling with the effort.

Suddenly she felt Liam's strong arms around her. He was rubbing her back and trying to soothe her. Liam was holding her against his chest and it felt so good to be held in his arms. It was like refuge from the storms of life.

"Ruby. Are you all right? You're scaring me."

"I saw it. In my mind's eye. It felt like I was reliving it. Rufus located several climbers who were trapped. And then he slipped off the ledge. I rappelled down to see if I could help him, but it was too late. And then I remember hearing this horrific noise. It was coming at me so fast…and then there was nothing. Just nothing. I was gone."

"It's going to be okay. You're safe now," he crooned as he caressed the side of her face and pulled her against his chest.

"I remember you walking with Rufus…and Aidan," she cried.

"It's good to remember, Ruby, but I don't want you going through this emotional turmoil. It can't be good for you."

She pulled away from him. "You can't protect me from this, Liam. It happened. I lived it. And through God's grace I survived it."

Liam shook his head. "My father blew into town like a tornado and stirred everything up. I never wanted you to have to relive your darkest moments."

"I can't pick and choose what I remember," she said with a shrug. "I'm actually grateful to Gareth. It's painful, but what I just remembered is a huge event. And it gives me hope that I can remember other crucial moments in my life. And who knows? Maybe I can return to search and rescue if I'm healthy enough to do so."

Liam's entire body stiffened. His expression darkened. "How can you even consider doing that? I won't let you put yourself in harm's way. It's not going to happen!"

Liam had just thrown down the gauntlet. It simmered in the air between them.

"If I ever decide to go back to search and rescue, that's my decision, Liam. I never gave you permission to run my life," she snapped.

Hurt flared in Liam's eyes. She hated to see that wounded look, but he'd cornered her and forced her to stand up for herself. Over the last two years she'd had to make decisions for herself in her day-to-day life. Liam couldn't expect to just step in and make all her choices for her, especially when it came to something as huge as her former career.

"Point taken, Ruby," Liam said in a clipped tone. "I'll remember next time not to care if you decide to put yourself in harm's way and make Aidan a motherless child all over again."

Ruby sucked in a shocked breath. Liam's words served as a punch in the gut. They bordered on being cruel. Deliberately hurtful.

Ruby turned away from Liam without a single word more and made a fast retreat to the guest bedroom. In the past few days it had felt as if they were growing ever closer, despite her stalled memories. Now, it seemed as if rushing rivers stood between them. And she had no idea how they were going to bridge the distance.

Chapter Nine

Liam settled into his seat at the Moose Café. He looked around the place, admiring the festive Christmas decorations that were now on full display. Sprigs of holly hung by the window while a fully decorated pine tree sat in the corner. Gaily wrapped presents were scattered beneath it. Holiday tunes softly emanated from speakers. Liam tapped his foot to the beat underneath the table.

The café really had become a favorite of almost everyone in Love. He admired his younger brother for reaching for the stars and making his dream come true.

As he did at least a few times a week, he was treating himself to lunch at his brother's establishment. He looked up at the door just in time to see Boone striding through with his best friend, Declan O'Rourke, by his side. Declan, Boone's lifelong best friend, was the owner and one of the pilots for O'Rourke Charters, a private plane company he ran out of Love. Just married to the town librarian, Annie Murray, Declan was an unofficial member of the Prescott family.

"Hey, Liam," Declan greeted him. "Thanks for the lunch invite."

"Hey, bro," Boone said as he settled into his chair. "I'm starved."

"You're always as hungry as a bear. Poor Grace must be sick of cooking for you," Liam said, chuckling. "She probably can't keep up."

Boone peered at his brother from behind the menu. "I cook just as many meals as Gracie. I consider myself a Renaissance man."

Liam and Declan looked at each other and burst out laughing.

Boone rolled his eyes. "Laugh all you want. You two could take pointers from me. Annie and Ruby would thank me for it."

Declan looked over at Liam. "How are things going, by the way? Is Ruby getting acclimated to town?"

"Honor invited Ruby and Aidan to the Wildlife Center today, so that'll be a fun trip." Liam frowned. "Everything was going pretty smoothly until we were blindsided by a visit from Pops yesterday."

Cameron walked up just at that moment. He stopped in his tracks and gaped at Liam. "Pops is here in Love?" He sank into a chair.

Liam swung his gaze up at his brother. "At least, he was last night. Sorry. I thought you knew."

Boone slapped the menu down on the table. "What did he want?"

"Not to catch up on all times, that's for sure." Liam drummed his fingers on the table. "He came for Ruby."

"Ruby?" Declan asked. "Gareth isn't the sentimental type. It's hard to believe he heard about Ruby and was so moved he came back home. That's not his style."

"Something tells me Liam has more to tell us," Boone drawled. "Spill it!"

"He came to find out if Ruby was fit to return to duty. He was flown here by his employer to ask Ruby if she wanted to return to search and rescue." He clenched his fists on the table. "It took every impulse in my body not to toss him out on his ear. He basically wanted to be able to go back and tell his bosses that Ruby was ready to go back to work."

Cameron scoffed. "Maybe he got a bonus or something out of it. Wonder if Jasper knows."

"This is so typical!" Boone snapped. "Did he even see Aidan or ask about Emma? He's never even met Gracie. He didn't show up at Cam's wedding or mine. And I'm not even sure he's aware that Honor is back in Love."

"You'd think one of these days he'd get his act together," Declan grumbled. "You guys know my dad isn't any better. At least Gareth shows up once in a blue moon."

Liam grunted. "To stir up a hornet's nest. Ruby and I got into it about the whole idea of her returning to search and rescue. It didn't end on a good note, I'm afraid."

"Did I miss something?" Cameron asked, a quizzical expression stamped on his face. "How can she resume that career with amnesia?"

"They were sending out feelers about her coming back down the road. That's the sense I got from his probing. Little by little, Ruby is remembering bits and pieces, so it's very possible. She remembered me and Aidan. She even had flashbacks about Rufus and what happened to him during the rescue."

"So I take it you would have a problem with her returning to search and rescue?" Boone asked, gazing at him intensely.

"Of course I would." Liam frowned. "It cost my family everything. We lost Ruby for two torturous years. The truth is, we might never fully get her back. We're still in limbo, Boone. And there's no guarantee that we're ever going to get back what we lost. Why would Ruby ever want to go down that road again?"

Boone held up his hands. "I see where you're coming from, but as a member of law enforcement, I just have to tell you that it seeps under our skin…it becomes part of our identity. Ruby may feel compelled to go back to service."

His brother's words were not the ones he wanted to hear. But he couldn't afford to ignore them. Boone was one of the smartest, most perceptive people he had ever known. He was his go-to person for advice. As always, his words were golden.

"What can I get y'all to eat?" Sophie chirped as she walked up to the table with a pencil and small pad in hand. "The salmon frittata with red potatoes on the side is real popular today. And Hazel is making a mean frozen hot chocolate with three types of chocolate."

"Sophie, I'm going to have the bison burger with truffle fries," Cameron said. "And a tall glass of water."

"Just a cup of the caribou stew and some flatbread," Boone said, sitting back in his chair and folding his arms across his chest. "Oh, and one of those frozen hot chocolates."

Liam smiled. When Cameron had first opened the Moose Café Boone had been skeptical of the specialty drinks. Now Boone considered himself a connoisseur of all the various drinks on the menu.

"I'll have the same," Declan added. "That'll really hit the spot. I have to make a run to Seward later on. I might stay over if the weather kicks up. There's a storm brewing."

"I'm going to have the turkey wrap with avocado and bacon," Liam said, looking up at Sophie, who was patiently waiting with a perky smile on her face. Matter of fact, Liam realized, he couldn't remember ever having seen Sophie without a sweet disposition. She was a true Georgia peach.

"You always order that," Sophie said with a grin. "Next time I'm going to skip asking you," she teased.

"I'm a man who knows what he wants," Liam quipped, handing the menu back to Sophie.

Sophie leaned down so only Liam could hear her. "I met Ruby at the tea party. She's everything I imagined she would be. I'm rooting for the two of you. Your family is in my prayers."

Liam reached out and squeezed Sophie's hand. "I appreciate that, Soph."

As Sophie walked away, Liam jutted his chin in her direction.

"That gal right there is some kind of wonderful," Liam said. He shook his head, buoyed by Sophie's heartwarming words. It helped to know that his family wasn't an island. Thoughts, prayers and well wishes all helped him feel as if the whole fishing village was pulling for them. Somehow it served to ease the pain of his father's actions. It let him know he wasn't alone.

"She sure is," Cameron agreed. "Whoever ends up with Sophie better treat her right."

"Yep," Declan agreed. "And if he doesn't, he's going to have to deal with us."

They nodded in unison, knowing that no one better toy with Sophie's heart. She was under their protection just as much as Honor. With a heart of gold, a pretty face and a sunny disposition, it would only be a matter of time.

"You know that we're here for you, Liam. This can't be easy," Boone said, his eyes full of concern. "You grieved for Ruby for a very long time. I know your emotions must be all over the place. Joy. Confusion. Anger."

Liam blew out a deep breath. Boone had hit the nail right on the head. So far, no one had really touched upon his feelings in all of this. Outside of being grateful and happy about Ruby's return, there were a host of other emotions he was battling. And he really didn't have an outlet. Between providing a strong foundation for Aidan, helping Ruby get her bearings, and taking care of his patients at the clinic, he really hadn't had time to process everything.

"Thanks. Honestly, I think part of me is still in shock. And you're right, it's confusing. I don't think that I realized how angry I was until Pops started pushing my buttons."

"Who are you upset with?" Cameron asked.

Liam shrugged. "I don't know. The whole situation, I suppose."

Cameron, Boone and Declan shared a glance loaded with meaning.

"What?" he asked, looking around the table.

"It seems like you might be mad at Ruby," Declan said. He held up his hands, as if to ward off Liam. "I could be wrong. Don't shoot the messenger."

Angry with Ruby? Why would he blame her for everything that had transpired two years ago? She was a victim. She had suffered more than anyone.

"No!" he protested. "That's not it."

"Give yourself a break, Liam," Cameron snapped. "You're human. Ruby worked in a dangerous field. I know you weren't always comfortable with it."

Liam's shoulders sagged. "And the award for worst husband goes to Dr. Liam Prescott." He shoved his hand through his hair. "On some level I suppose I am angry that Ruby went on the search and rescue when it was something we had argued about."

"Don't say that you're a bad husband," Boone chided. "You've been the most loving, faithful partner in the world. Because of the way you two honored and respected each other, you made me believe that maybe someday I could have a love like that. And then I found Gracie." Boone's voice softened. "So don't ever say that...not when I'm around."

Liam was touched. Boone had never told him before that his relationship with Ruby had inspired him. Despite their fractured upbringing, the Prescott siblings had always shared a tight bond. And they had all idolized Boone, who had been their hero. To know that he had been a source of hope for his brother made Liam feel ten feet tall. He had given something back to Boone to repay him in some small way for everything he had done for him.

Boone's poignant words served to remind him of everything he should be fighting tooth and nail to preserve. So far he had been allowing fear to guide him. He hadn't been giving it his all with Ruby. He was so afraid of being rejected by her again that he had lost sight of everything they had been to one another. Rather than focus on the love, he had spent too much time dissecting the things that had gone wrong between them.

"I've got your drinks. Waters for everyone and two frozen hot chocolates!" Sophie said as she returned and placed the drinks on the table.

"Did I interrupt something?" Sophie asked as she looked around at them.

"No," Liam said, feeling humbled by Boone's words and the support offered by Cameron and Declan. "Boone was just reminding me of how blessed I am. Sometimes we lose sight of it for different reasons, but my big brother just gave me a reality check."

"That's what big brothers are for," Boone drawled. A wide grin broke out over his face.

Liam couldn't stop thinking about Ruby. His sweet, beautiful wife. He had been so out of sorts last night that he hadn't even allowed himself to rejoice at the fact that Ruby now had memories related to him. Real, tangible moments.

Despite their argument, Liam felt hopeful. There

was nothing they couldn't fix if they worked toward that goal with hope and faith.

"Do you guys mind if I bail on lunch? I have the afternoon free," Liam asked as the germ of an idea began to percolate in his mind. "I think it might be nice to surprise my family at the Wildlife Center."

"Good call," Boone said with an approving grin.

"Better than sitting around with these two mugs," Cameron drawled, earning himself a jab in the side from Declan.

After saying his goodbyes, he jumped up from his seat and asked Sophie to wrap his sandwich as a to-go meal. As he left the Moose Café, Liam began to fervently pray.

Dear Lord. Please help me bridge the gap between Ruby and me. I don't want to walk in fear anymore. The past shouldn't be something to be afraid of. You have given us this wondrous gift. I want to celebrate Ruby's return without looking over my shoulder.

"I'm so excited! I can't wait to see Auntie Honor's animals."

Aidan's enthusiastic voice from the back seat served as a joyful reminder of what this outing was all about. Although she was curious about Honor's job and the animals, her true joy would be in seeing it all through her son's eyes. He was rapidly becoming the center of her world.

"This is a real treat for us," Ruby said, observing him in the rearview mirror. "Don't forget to thank Honor for inviting us."

“I won’t,” Aidan chirped, sounding like a contented baby bird.

She wished that her current mood was more in line with Aidan’s cheerful outlook on life. Ruby didn’t know how to explain the feelings coursing through her. Ever since the blowup with Liam yesterday, her mind felt like mush. She kept replaying it over and over again in her mind, wondering where she’d gone wrong. She had acted on instinct and stood up for herself. Liam had been tense and moody. Ruby still felt furious about his comment regarding Aidan. Her whole body tightened just thinking about it.

Why did she feel so out of sorts? People argued. But by all accounts, she and Liam had been sheer perfection together. She bit her lip, wondering if the conflict between them stemmed from her. After all, she wasn’t the same Ruby. Not really.

Her chest tightened painfully at the thought of Liam. Although she was still angry at him, a part of her wished he was here with them. The word *heartsick* came to mind. It didn’t make sense since she wasn’t in love with Liam, but she couldn’t ignore that her feelings for him were growing by leaps and bounds. Perhaps that was the reason for her feeling ill at ease. She was beginning to care for him, and the harsh words they had exchanged yesterday put them at odds.

She knew she should just live in the moment. Her therapist in Colorado had taught her how to focus on living in the here and now rather than dwelling on the past. That’s what she needed to do right now instead of rehashing the terrible scene with her husband. She prayed that God would help them fix things.

Ruby let out a sigh of appreciation as the stunning Alaskan vista began to unfold around her. They were heading into a more remote area of Love where signs of habitation were scarce. Gigantic, snow-covered trees dominated the scenery. Mountains were so close she felt as if she could reach out and touch them. There were no houses or shops or cute little cafés that served up coffee drinks. Honor's wildlife center was in the boondocks.

As they pulled into the entrance, Ruby noticed the stallions in the paddock. They were beautiful, graceful animals, roaming wild and free in the snow. She slowed the car so Aidan could get a good look. He oohed and aahed from the back seat, making her chuckle with his over-the-top appreciation of the horses.

Ruby followed the signs along the way, turning left to continue on toward the main house.

Before they had even exited the car, Honor came running out of the ranch-style house. Dressed casually in blue jeans, a brightly colored T-shirt and a bomber-style jacket, she looked relaxed and enthused.

"Welcome!" she said, extending her arms wide. Aidan ran straight toward her and catapulted himself into her arms. "Hey, buddy. I'm so glad you guys came by today."

Honor, with her fresh-faced beauty, chestnut-colored hair and warm blue-gray eyes looked radiant.

"Thank you for inviting us, Auntie Honor," Aidan said, looking over at Ruby for confirmation he'd done a good job of following her instructions.

Ruby smiled at him, sending him an encouraging nod. “Aidan almost couldn’t sleep last night. He was so excited. And to be honest, so am I.”

“I hope you didn’t have any trouble finding this place,” Honor said, reaching out and touching her arm.

“Not at all,” Ruby said. “I had my GPS and a set of directions I printed out. It gave me an opportunity to really enjoy the scenery.”

“Well, you two made my day by coming to visit. I love it out here, but it does get a bit lonely.”

“But you have the animals,” Aidan chimed in. “Don’t they keep you company?”

“You’re right about that, Aidan. The only problem is that they don’t talk to me when I ask them things,” she said with a chuckle.

“What animals do you have here?” Aidan asked, looking around him as if he expected one to pop up right before his eyes.

Honor bent so she was eye-level with her nephew. She reached out and pulled his hat down over his ears. “So far we have eagles, wolves, moose, foxes and a lot more. Why don’t I show you around and you can see for yourself?”

“Sounds like a plan.” Ruby zipped up her coat. The December temperature had dipped even lower than it had been over the last few days. She glanced over at Aidan. His coat wasn’t fastened all the way up. She reached over and adjusted it so that his neck wasn’t exposed. Alaskan weather was no joke. Hypothermia could set in at any time of the year, mostly when the temps were between thirty and fifty degrees Fahrenheit.

Hmm. How do I know that? She smiled at the realization that more and more information was coming back to her.

All of a sudden they heard the low rumbling of an engine and the sound of tires crunching on the snow-packed road. Honor raised her hand to shade her eyes from the sun.

"That's Liam's car," she announced, turning toward Ruby and Aidan. A smile lit her face.

"Daddy!" Aidan called out.

Ruby felt her pulse skitter. She wasn't sure what emotion was roaring through her as she watched Liam step out of the car. Aidan ran toward him at breakneck speed then jumped into his father's arms. Ruby placed her hand on her stomach as butterflies did somersaults at the sight of the two of them.

As if in slow motion, Liam walked toward them, Aidan at his side. As he got closer, he locked eyes with her and she felt something shift inside her. It felt so right to have him standing there with them. She couldn't put her feelings into words, but despite everything brewing between them, she always felt better being in Liam's presence. Safer. More grounded.

"Hey! We weren't expecting you," Honor said. "I was just about to give the tour."

Liam still hadn't taken his eyes off Ruby. "Great! There's no place I'd rather be."

She looked away, feeling nervous at the intensity of his gaze. The heated exchange from yesterday still stood between them.

"Well, let's get started, then," Honor said, the corners of her mouth twitching in amusement.

Aidan planted himself right next to Honor, while Liam walked beside her. With his long legs, Ruby knew instinctively that he was slowing his gait so he didn't outpace her. Silence stretched between them for a few moments.

"I'm glad you decided to come," Ruby blurted. "You should have seen Aidan's face when you pulled up."

"Me, too," Liam said with a nod. "I've been here before, but Aidan's never gotten the full tour. There's nothing better than seeing something through a child's eyes."

"So, what determines which animals come to the center?" Ruby asked.

"The Wildlife Center takes in orphaned and injured animals. The goal is to rehabilitate them so they can go back into the wild," Liam explained.

"It's very important work," Ruby said, feeling very grateful to Honor for giving them the grand tour and giving them an up-close and personal look at something so special to her.

"It sure is," Liam acknowledged. "And she was born to do this."

Honor and Aidan stopped up ahead to wait for them as they reached the first structure.

"Come on, slowpokes," Aidan called out, waving them on with his arm.

As soon as they caught up, Honor ushered them toward the white, ranch-style building.

"Let's check out the aviary. I'll show you our newest friend," Honor said.

As soon as they stepped inside, Honor led them to an area where they could see the enclosure through a glass window. A gorgeous bald eagle sat on the ground, pecking at something in a round bowl.

"Cool!" Aidan shouted, pressing his nose against the glass.

"This is Dolly. She's a bald eagle with a severely injured wing. She can't fend for herself out in the wild due to her injuries, so we're taking care of her until she can do it for herself."

"What happened to her? Did a coyote get her?" Aidan asked.

"No, Aidan," Honor said in a solemn voice. "A bullet pierced Dolly's wing. We're hoping it gets better so she can learn to fly again."

"I can't believe someone would do that," Ruby said. "Aren't eagles on the endangered species list?"

"Not anymore," Liam said. "Although it's still illegal to try to harm them."

"We need to care for animals," Aidan said. "Like we did for Rufus."

"I can't believe you remember him," Ruby said. "You were just a little one then."

"I was almost three when he died, but I remember him giving me kisses and going for walks in the woods with him." Aidan looked up at her, affection shining in his eyes. "I remember loving him."

"So do I," she whispered as she nuzzled Aidan's cheek with her gloved hand. Being here at the center was bringing into focus her own love of animals, dogs in particular.

As they walked around the wildlife preserve, Ruby found herself in awe of Honor's knowledge. Honor explained to her that she had a master's degree in wildlife biology. To open the wildlife center, permission had to be granted by Alaska's Department of Fish and Game. Finding a visionary who could make it happen had been key.

"Opening this center was always my dream. Funding was the hard part. I'm fortunate to have partnered with people who really believe in conservation and animal activism. They put their money where their hearts lie. This place still needs the generosity of donors, though. We're hoping to have some fund-raisers across the state to ensure future programs."

For the next few hours Honor showed them around. They were able to get a glimpse of a wide variety of animals—bison, birds, wolves, baby elk, a sitka black-tailed deer, moose. Aidan was able to pet a baby wolf named Hercules who had been found abandoned in the woods.

"Do you have any dogs?" Aidan crossed his hands prayerfully in front of him as he asked the question.

"We do have a few. Let's go meet Rita." Honor led them toward an area where four dogs were in an enclosure. Three of them were running around and playing with each other while the fourth one was peacefully lying on a mat. Once they entered the enclosure all the dogs came running toward them. Ruby found herself being greeted enthusiastically by a black-and-white terrier who was missing a leg. His name tag read Diego in big letters. Ruby placed her arms around him and hugged him. The sound of Aidan's hearty chuckle rang out as Diego began licking her face.

Ruby felt the heat of Liam's gaze as he watched her bond with the dog.

How could she ever have forgotten how good it felt to be around dogs?

"Rita is about to have a litter of babies," Honor explained, moving toward the golden retriever reclining on the mat. "Any day now."

"Like Aunt Gracie?" Aidan asked, his brown eyes wide. He began patting Rita on the head.

Honor, Liam and Ruby burst out laughing. Out of the mouths of babes.

"Sort of, but not really. Rita is going to have several at one time and we're going to have to find homes for them," Honor explained. "Grace is expecting only one, unless they're holding out on us."

"Can we take one of the puppies, Dad? Pretty please with sugar on top." Aidan held his hands in front of him, crossing them in prayerful fashion.

Liam's expression was conflicted. "I don't know, Aidan. We have a lot going on at the moment and puppies are a lot of work."

"Please," he begged, shifting his eyes toward Ruby. "I'll feed him and walk him and teach him a bunch of tricks."

Liam turned toward her. He knit his brows together. "What do you think?"

Personally, she would love to own another dog, but

Ruby wasn't sure she should even weigh in on it. So much about the future was uncertain. Would she be remaining in Love? If she and Liam couldn't even agree on her career, how would their marriage survive the challenge of her amnesia?

And there was still so much tension lingering between them from yesterday.

"I think it's something we should talk about at greater length," she said in a halting voice. She looked down at Aidan. Her heart sank as she recognized the signs of his vast disappointment. His lower lip trembled while his shoulders sagged. She bent over and tipped up his chin, so she could look him in the eye. Tears shimmered in his warm brown eyes.

"I know that's not what you want to hear," she said in a soft voice, "but bringing a pet into the home is serious business. Do you know that a lot of people make impulsive decisions to bring dogs home and then it doesn't work out? This isn't a no, it's simply a let's wait and see."

"I think that makes a lot of sense," Liam said with a nod.

"Why don't we head back to the main house for hot chocolate?" Honor suggested. Aidan's mood turned on a dime. Ruby sent her a grateful look for diverting her son's attention away from Rita and her soon-to-be brood.

Ruby was certain that Aidan's shouts of glee could be heard all the way back in town. As she walked hand in hand with Aidan as they journeyed back across the property, Ruby felt lighter and more joyful than she had in ages. The beauty of this day hadn't allowed her to dwell on the tension between her and Liam. It seemed that both of them had tried to put it aside so they could enjoy the Wildlife Center as a family.

Each day was bringing something new and wonderful her way. She just needed to look closely enough to see it. And to embrace the little boy who had swiftly stolen her heart.

Thank You, Lord. For gifting us with this wondrous day.

Chapter Ten

Later on that evening, Ruby stood at the sink washing dinner dishes. Her back was turned to Liam. He silently admired the graceful slope of her neck and the tiny little curls that had escaped her bun. She was radiant, even in all her simplicity. Her jeans and plaid-flannel T-shirt did nothing to diminish it. If anything, it only served to highlight it.

Liam still hadn't broached the subject of their disagreement from yesterday. Even though things had thawed between them this afternoon, the situation didn't rest easy on his heart. God had given him the tremendous gift of bringing Ruby back into his life and now he was squandering it.

He'd given it a lot of thought this afternoon. He could have handled the situation better, yet he'd lost control of his emotions and alienated Ruby in the process. Something had to give. They couldn't continue living under the same roof and walking on eggshells all the time.

Liam moved toward the kitchen counter. He stood

close to her so that their arms were slightly touching. Her nearness caused a yearning he had stuffed down inside him for ages. The smell of lavender drifted toward him, causing him to take a good whiff of her light perfume. It was torture to be so close to his beautiful wife and not take her in his arms. So far he had reined himself in, but he didn't know how long he could continue to do so.

"Nice day out at the Wildlife Center," he remarked in a casual tone.

She nodded without looking at him. "Yes, it was."

"Don't you think we should talk?" Liam slightly raised his voice over the sound of the water from the sink.

"About what?" Ruby asked without turning around or shutting off the water. She continued to scrub the dishes.

"You're still angry with me. I get that. But we have to extend each other an olive branch. Sooner or later Aidan will pick up on the tension between us."

Ruby snapped her head in his direction. "That's a cheap shot, throwing Aidan into the situation."

"It happens to be the truth," he said in a curt voice. "Don't be so prickly about everything just because you're upset with me."

Ruby bristled. "I don't like being angry. It doesn't sit well with me."

"I don't like seeing you this way, either," he admitted. "It's not your way."

She turned off the water and wiped her hands on a dish towel. "I'm not backing down from my stance," she said. Her expression showed a fierceness he hadn't seen since she had returned. It was classic Ruby.

"Neither am I," he replied. "I've always done what's

best for our family. You may have been the professional at saving lives, but I've always served and protected our family."

She folded her arms across her chest. "We can agree to disagree. Life's too short to harbor grudges or carry around negative energy."

"I agree. I know what it feels like to have the bottom fall out of my world in an instant. It feels silly to waste time being angry at each other."

"Ditto," she said.

She bowed her head. "But I'm still bent out of shape about the way you acted the other day. Not only toward me, but your father, as well."

His father? There wasn't time enough in the world for him to explain all the nuances of their fractured relationship. As a result, he looked like the bad guy in the situation.

"I've always regarded myself as your protector. Old habits die hard."

"Being protective is one thing, but bossing me around is another. Something tells me you didn't get away with that before the accident. Am I right?"

"You always gave as good as you got," he admitted. "You've never been the backing down type." They both laughed, which managed to ease the lingering tension a little bit.

"That's good to know," Ruby said.

"I'm sorry about what I said about you leaving Aidan motherless. It wasn't right." Just remembering his dig made his skin crawl. There had been some truth in his statement, but he'd known it would hurt Ruby to utter those words. That alone made him feel ashamed.

"Apology accepted," she said with a nod. "I would never willingly hurt Aidan. And I have to live with the fact that the repercussions of my career choices left him motherless for a time." She quirked her mouth. "Honestly, I didn't really need the reminder."

"Losing you in a rescue mission…that was always my worst fear. Then it happened. And just the thought of what might happen if you go back to search and rescue makes me crazy." He shuddered. "It plays on all those fears and the nightmare we've already lived through."

Ruby nodded. "I get where you're coming from, but it still isn't something you can lecture me against doing. That's not going to fly with me."

Although Liam liked the way Ruby was standing up for herself in true Ruby fashion, he hated that she was sticking to her guns about the possibility of returning to her career. As far as he was concerned, it was a no-brainer. Hadn't they decided Aidan's needs came first? Why tempt fate? They had already been put through the ringer because of her job.

Rather than stir up the hornet's nest any further, he needed to get a few things off his chest about his father. The topic of Gareth Prescott was one he usually avoided like the plague. But he needed Ruby to know where he was coming from so she didn't write him off as a jerk.

"With regard to my father, the friction between us goes back a long time. Whether you realize it or not, he came here with an agenda, Ruby. And that is galling to me, considering he was MIA for the past two years. Not once did he ever call to check in on us. Not an email or a text or a letter. Not even a smoke signal." He let out a harsh laugh. "And when Jasper had a heart attack, it barely registered with him."

"I'm sorry, Liam. That sounds awful. Has it always been like this?" Ruby asked, her expression radiating compassion.

"Pretty much," Liam admitted. Even though he had convinced himself over the years it no longer hurt, the piercing sensation near his stomach proved otherwise. Even as an adult, Gareth Prescott still managed to tie him up in knots.

"When my parents divorced, neither one of them put their children first. Jasper became our surrogate parent and he did right by us. When Boone became an adult, he took all of us under his wing. He helped me foot the bill for medical school. He played the role of surrogate father. Neither of my parents were the warm and fuzzy type. And the truth is, they have both kept a far distance from us. It hasn't been easy for any of us, but Honor had it the worst since she's the youngest."

"I'm sorry," Ruby whispered. "It's unfathomable to me that parents would act like that."

"It is what it is," Liam said with a sigh. "All the Prescott siblings have had to come to terms with it the best we can. I think when they divorced they both decided they wanted to be footloose and fancy free. No real attachments or responsibilities."

"For the life of me I can't imagine that," Ruby murmured.

"When we got married I stressed the part about sticking it out because I came from the opposite of that. More than anything, I believe in honoring the commitments we make in this life…to each other and Aidan and our faith." In a strange way Liam felt as if he had just laid his heart down on the table for Ruby to dissect. He had told her in a nutshell his belief system and what mattered to him most of all. As a man who tended to go inward, it was a huge deal for him.

"Thank you for telling me about Gareth. I see why it was so tense the day he was here. I can't blame you for questioning his showing up here unannounced after he'd pretty much bailed out of your life."

"I appreciate your listening. As the saying goes, we can't pick our parents. On the flip side, it made me want to be everything I could be in Aidan's world because I never had it."

"And you are," Ruby said with a smile. "Watching the two of you together is such a joyful experience. You've done such a great job raising him."

"Being his father has been such a gift," Liam said, his voice breaking a little. When God had blessed him with the gift of fatherhood, it had been the greatest day of his life. He had never taken the responsibility lightly. And he never would.

Ruby bit her lip and ducked her head. She seemed to be having a moment of shyness. "I know things have been tense between us, but I wanted you to know that I had some flashes of you, in addition to the ones involving Rufus. Something opened up in me that day when Gareth visited. I remember the two of us being on a mountain and sledding down a hill. You were laughing and teasing me. You threw a snowball at me and it hit me right on the nose."

Raw emotion rose inside Liam. He remembered that day, as well. It had been one of the best days of his life. "We were out at Deer Lake. That afternoon you told me that you were expecting Aidan." He let out a ragged sigh. "Not many things in this life can ever compare to that moment."

"We were happy, weren't we?" she asked.

"Yes, we were, Ruby. I'd never call us perfect, but we sure had a great life. We laughed and we loved and we worked hard to build a life for ourselves."

And it had been truly wonderful. He wasn't exaggerating. They had been best friends. Co-parents. Two people who had been committed to living out their lives together with their son. Difficult times had come, but he'd never thought for a single moment those times had defined them.

A hint of a smile played around her lips. She twirled a strand of her hair around her finger. "That feels reassuring to me to hear you say that. It fills in the gaps."

"I'm going to call Honor and see if she can watch Aidan tomorrow night." Liam threw the comment out casually.

She frowned at him. "Why do you need a sitter?"

The idea had been percolating for a while now, but he knew this would be the perfect time to put his plan in motion. So far he hadn't been able to spend much quality time around Ruby without Aidan being present. And although he loved his son dearly, he wanted "alone time" with his wife. They needed it.

"Because I want to take you out on a date tomorrow night, Ruby. A good, old-fashioned date. How do you feel about that?"

A date with her husband? After all the tension between them, it was the last thing she had expected to hear Liam say. How did she feel about it? Excited. Nervous. It was thrilling. But she wanted to try to keep her cool and not act too giddy about it.

"That sounds nice," she had answered with a smile.

"Good. Tomorrow night at seven o'clock. Dinner."

Now, almost twenty-four hours later, she was doing her very best to make herself look date-worthy. With Liam's help, she had moved a lot of her personal items, including clothes, into the guest bedroom, so she was able to look through her wardrobe for an outfit to wear.

After narrowing her choice to three outfits, she settled on a burgundy wool dress that was flattering to her figure and stylish. She experimented with her hair, using the curling iron to create long, loose waves. Dangling earrings gave the ensemble a little pizazz. Having never mastered the art of makeup in the last two years, Ruby decided to stick with a mauve shade of lipstick and some mascara. She studied herself with a critical eye.

Yes, indeed. She sure cleaned up well. Hopefully, Liam would agree.

She smoothed her hand over her stomach. Butterflies were flip-flopping around inside, a direct result of her sudden case of jitters. This date was everything to her. It was an opportunity to test the waters with Liam, to see if these feelings brewing between them could serve as a foundation for the future. To know whether there was truly a place for her in this wonderful Alaskan community.

There was no need to be a bundle of nerves. This was Liam. She knew him. He wasn't just some stranger who had popped up in her life. She had strong, joyful memories of him. Each day more moments from the past were coming back to her.

And even if she hadn't recovered a few memories of her husband, he'd showed her in the here and now that he was a wonderful, kindhearted man. A giving man. Wasn't that the most important thing of all?

A few times she had answered the landline and spoken to patients seeking out Dr. Liam Prescott. Ruby didn't know of any doctors who regularly gave out their home phone number for emergencies. Each and every time, Liam had taken the call and spoken to the caller with compassion and warmth.

It was starting to feel like she had a crush on her own husband.

The sound of the doorbell ringing intruded upon her thoughts. A quick glance at her watch showed it was almost seven o'clock. When the pealing of the bell continued, she left the guest room and headed toward the front door. Who could it be? Honor was already inside, eating macaroni and cheese in the kitchen with Aidan. It was a little bit odd that Aidan hadn't run to the door to open it. More times than not, that's what he did.

Ruby swung the door open, letting out a squeak when Liam's tall frame filled the doorway.

"Good evening," he drawled, handing her a bouquet

of white roses, baby's breath and red carnations. He was dressed in a dark jacket paired with a white shirt and a tan pair of slacks. He looked simply divine. She discreetly sniffed the air around them. He smelled pine-fresh like the great outdoors.

"Aren't you going to invite me in?" he asked, his lips twitching with merriment.

"Seriously?" she blurted. He was standing there looking handsome and swoon-worthy and capable of completely sweeping her off her feet.

He grinned, showcasing his perfect set of pearly whites. "Yes, seriously. This is a first-date move. Since you can't remember our real first date, I figured we should make this the first one. As I recall, I showed up at your apartment and rang your bell, presented you with flowers and took you out on the town."

If she hadn't already had a major-league crush on Liam, this would have pushed her straight over the edge. She ushered him in, firmly closing the door behind him. When she turned back to him, he was standing mere inches from her, staring her down with his magnetic blue eyes.

"You look amazing." Liam's eyes were full of appreciation as he looked her up and down, his gaze lingering a few beats too long. Something hummed and buzzed in the air—an awareness that felt palpable.

"Thank you," she murmured. "You don't look half bad yourself."

Suddenly, Honor and Aidan were standing there, grinning from ear to ear.

Ruby placed her hand on her hip. "I suppose the two of you were in on this, huh?" she asked.

"Yep," Aidan said. "Auntie Honor said it was romantic." Aidan made a face.

Ruby felt her cheeks blushing. It had been terribly romantic.

"Let me take your flowers and put them in a vase while you get your coat and purse," Honor suggested. She reached for the bouquet and pressed it to her nose. "If I can find a guy who'll give me flowers and moonlight, I might just marry him."

Although Honor's tone was teasing, Ruby sensed something lying behind her words. A true yearning to be connected with someone, she imagined.

After getting her purse and coat, Ruby joined Liam in the living room where they said their goodbyes to Aidan and Honor. As they set off into the freezing-cold night, Ruby couldn't resist asking Liam where they were headed.

"There's a restaurant over by the pier that only opens for dinner service. We used to be regulars there. It's called The Bay."

"So why only dinner service?" Ruby asked, feeling curious about the place.

"The owners are getting a little on in years. They came here from Italy more than thirty years ago. It was their dream to open a restaurant here and they did. But a few years ago this town had a recession. Everyone was hurting. Sal and Renata had to cut back their service to only one a day." He glanced over at her and smiled.

"And the funny thing is they're doing better now than ever, since they streamlined the business."

"That's fantastic," Ruby said as she looked out the window at the scenery whizzing by. "I love hearing success stories like that."

"Me, too. It reminds me of Cameron. It took a tremendous amount of courage for him to open the Moose Café. He was coming off a huge town scandal involving Paige's father and embezzlement of town funds. There were a lot of naysayers."

"I'm sad he had to go through that, but I'm really happy he prevailed in the end. He and Paige and Emma seem so happy."

"They are. It hasn't been an easy road, though. They've endured a lot, but they've come out on the other side," Liam said. He turned off the road and entered a small parking lot near the pier. A red house glowing with brilliant lights stood about fifty feet away. A large tree decorated with twinkling ornaments stood in front of the farmhouse-style house.

Liam placed his hand on the small of her back and led her inside. The interior was packed with customers. It almost seemed as if every single table was occupied. Fantastic scents wafted in the air. The clanging of glasses and cutlery rang out.

"Liam! Nice to see you here." An older man with salt-and-pepper hair and a large frame greeted them. He locked gazes with her, then reached out and grabbed her by the arm. "Ruby! I'm Sal Terrazo. This is my place. And I'm very honored to have you here tonight. Let me show you to your table." He held out his elbow so Ruby could loop her arm through it. Once they arrived at the table, he pulled out her chair for her and then placed her napkin in her lap with a flourish.

"Your waiter will be over shortly. If the two of you need anything at all, don't hesitate to tell me." With a slight bow, he disappeared from the table.

Ruby almost gasped out loud when she realized they were seated right by the window overlooking Kachemak Bay. It was easily the best table in the whole place.

"Did you bribe someone for this spot?" she teased.

Liam flashed a knowing smile. "I didn't have to. Let's just say that the owners are the founding members of the Ruby Prescott Fan Club. They were more than happy to provide us with this incredible view."

She shook her head. "This is really nice. I wasn't expecting anything this incredible. Sal is amazing."

"He really is. There's a better view in the daytime, but there's something about the way the lights radiate off the water that really is spectacular." He peered out the window and pointed. "You can even see the mountains in the distance."

"I know this place," she blurted. "We had our first date here, didn't we?"

Liam nodded. "I can't believe you remember."

"It's hard sometimes because I'm not always sure if I'm remembering or if it's just a feeling. I do know this place, though. I remember eating pasta…lots and lots of pasta. And someone was teasing us about getting married one day. But that's all I remember."

Liam groaned. "That was Sal. Not exactly what a

girl wants to hear on a first date. But you let me take you out on a second one and then a third."

"And we fell in love." Her words were a statement rather than a question. Those tender moments still eluded her. More than anything, she wanted to know how they'd fallen for one another.

"When we fell in love, I was the skeptic. It comes from having two parents who couldn't honor their commitment to one another. It made me very leery of relationships." He laughed—a rich, deep laugh that seemed to rumble through his chest. "But you came crashing into my life with your open heart and optimism. Even though I half expected you to break my heart into a million little pieces, I couldn't not be with you. I was a goner—right from the start."

Hearing about their early beginnings made her feel emotional. "Thanks for sharing that with me, Liam. I wish I could remember that night in vivid detail."

Liam locked eyes with her. "I have full confidence that one of these days you will."

He believed in her, supported her attempts at recovering her memories. He was her husband and the father of her child. In another life she had loved this man. And at this very moment she felt a gigantic shift in her heart. It was opening up—to Dr. Liam Prescott and all the possibilities a life with him would mean for her.

If only she could be brave enough to reach out and grab it with both hands.

As Liam drove away from the waterfront after a spectacular dinner with Ruby, he found himself not wanting the evening to end. He hadn't even admitted it to himself over the years, but he had missed female companionship. Not just any female. He'd missed Ruby. The love of his life. And despite the fact she wasn't a carbon copy of the woman she had once been, there was still a huge part of her that had stayed the same. His heart recognized her.

And being afraid of being hurt by her seemed shallow in the scheme of things. God had brought Ruby back to them and she had fought her fears and doubts to journey to Love. Couldn't he muster the courage to do the same?

She turned toward him as she sat in the passenger seat. "Thanks for showing me such a great time, Liam. It was a very special night."

He glanced at her, overwhelmed by her beauty set against the soft interior glow of the truck.

"You're very welcome," he said, feeling relieved that Ruby had enjoyed the evening as much as he had. "It's still pretty early. We could go to the Moose for a cappuccino. They're extending their hours of operation for the holidays. I think Cameron has a band from Kodiak playing there tonight."

"I'd love to. That sounds fun."

Liam made a left onto Jarvis Street and found parking a few spots down from the café. He walked around to the passenger side and helped Ruby down from the truck. On impulse he reached for her hand. He walked slowly with her, pausing to point out Christmas displays in various windows. He showed her the red toboggan, and she agreed that Aidan would love it.

On impulse, he pulled her into the alcove of a storefront. She looked at him with questions brimming in her eyes.

"I know you don't remember it, but we kissed on our first date."

Ruby smiled at him. "I kissed you on our first date?"

"Yes, you did," Liam said, trying to keep his voice solemn. "I seem to remember you saying something about me being irresistible."

"It would seem you have me at a distinct disadvantage, since I can't remember our first kiss," Ruby said in a light voice.

"I remember it vividly," he said.

She shook her head and laughed, her long tresses swaying with the movement.

"So, Ruby Prescott, in the event that you're really opposed to being kissed by me, I'm letting you know right here and now that I'm going to kiss you." He reached out and traced the outline of her full, soft lips with his thumb. He didn't think he could wait a second longer. It already felt like an eternity since their lips had met.

"Okay," she whispered. Her brown eyes were looking up at him with such a wealth of emotion. One step and he would tumble right over the edge into their depths.

He leaned down and placed his lips over hers. *Take it slow*, he had to remind himself. This kiss had been a long time coming. Liam reached out and gently pulled her closer to him. Her lips were warm and inviting despite the frosty December temperature. The heady scent of lavender surrounded her. She was kissing him back with such tenderness it made him ache inside. He felt powerful emotions roar through him. His heart was soaring well past the safe boundaries he'd set for himself. It was way too late to guard his heart against this.

Ruby. His sweet, unforgettable Ruby.

"Liam," she murmured against his lips as the kiss ended. He laid his forehead against hers, wanting to stretch out the moment until the stars were stamped from the sky.

Ruby couldn't seem to stop thinking about the kiss she'd shared with Liam. She replayed it in her mind during the rest of the walk to the Moose Café, going over every nuance and small detail. Liam had been so tender and romantic. Her heart had done somersaults. It was her first kiss, after all, since she couldn't remember another. And as first kisses went, it had been spectacular. Ruby had wanted it to go on and on, to savor the tender moment for as long as possible. She had known in the moments before he'd dipped his head that Liam was going to kiss her. Truthfully, she'd been praying he would do so.

Liam had kissed her! And she had joyfully kissed him back. His lips had tasted like cinnamon and sugar. His arms had been steady and sure. He smelled like fresh pine. And for the life of her, she couldn't stop thinking about kissing him again.

From what she'd observed so far, Liam Prescott was a good man. Honorable. Faithful. True. And with every passing day, he was nestling himself further and further into her heart. The kiss had just solidified everything. Back in Denver she had dreamed about finding a man to share her life with. She had prayed to God to send her someone strong and loving and kind. Ruby looked up at the incandescent moon and felt a sweeping, soaring feeling rise inside her. At this moment she felt so happy she could almost soar as if on wings.

By the time Liam grasped her hand in his, Ruby wasn't certain she could contain her feelings. She felt as if she might burst with happiness.

"You're pretty quiet all of a sudden." Liam's deep voice intruded on her thoughts.

She looked over at him, admiring his strong jawline and the proud tilt of his head. Dr. Liam Prescott was an Alaskan hottie. And he was hers. All hers.

"I'm happy," she said, knowing she was beaming. "Thank you for this wonderful night."

Liam looked down at her, his handsome face lit with the same joy she felt. "The night's still young, Ruby." As he opened the door to the Moose Café and led her inside, Ruby found herself wishing that the happiness she felt at this very moment could last a lifetime.

Chapter Eleven

Considering it was a weeknight, the Moose was jumping. Although it was a tight crowd, Hazel managed to finagle a table for them so they could watch the show. Paige sat and joined them while Cameron was behind the scenes trying to ensure everything ran smoothly. The band from Kodiak had a big following, according to Paige. Cameron had said that some of their fans had even followed them to this gig in Love.

During the intermission, Cameron also came to join them at their table. He leaned over and pressed a kiss on his wife's forehead. It wasn't long before Hazel had pulled up a chair beside them.

"The band is the best we've had so far. And this place is filled to capacity." Cameron's face was lit like a kid in a candy store. Liam's chest swelled with pride. His brother had made lemonade out of lemons and earned his success through ingenuity and hard work. Now he was reaping the rewards.

"Proud of you," Liam said with a nod in his brother's direction.

All of a sudden Jasper came barreling through the door like a man on a mission. His hair was sticking up and his expression bordered on wild. He reached their table in a few determined strides.

"All right, woman. I surrender." Jasper held his hands up in the air. His voice was as loud as a foghorn.

Hazel gaped at him. "What are you talking about? Did you rob a bank or something?"

He heaved a tremendous sigh as if he was carrying the weight of the world on his shoulders. "You've hounded, harassed, intimidated, finagled and bamboozled me all in your quest to coerce me into putting a ring on your finger." He dug in his pocket and pulled out a wooden box. After fumbling with it for a few seconds he managed to prop it open. A beautiful diamond ring sat inside.

Hazel's jaw dropped. She muttered something unintelligible.

Liam leaned in toward Ruby. "Oh, no. This is not going to end well," he whispered. Liam made a slashing motion against his neck in the hope that Jasper would see his gesture and figure out his message.

Ruby bit her lip and looked at him with big eyes. "This is not the sort of proposal a woman dreams about," she whispered back. "It's really a stinker."

All Liam could do was shake his head.

Everything hushed and stilled in the Moose Café. Everyone seemed to sense that a tornado was brewing. It was a good thing he and Ruby had decided to come by the café tonight. Jasper might very well need medical attention when Hazel got through with him.

Hazel stood and raised up to her full height. She was face-to-face with Jasper. "I've waited my whole life for this moment. I thought it would happen in my twenties, prayed it might happen in my thirties and despaired of it ever happening in my forties. Then in my late fifties I met you and I started to hope again. I fell in love with an ornery codger who can't seem to see the forest for the trees. And up until this very moment, I was willing to forgive your idiosyncrasies. Jasper Alistair Prescott, I wouldn't marry you if you were the last bachelor in Love, Alaska. I might not have all the answers, but I do know one thing for certain." She sneered at him. "I deserve way better than a bootleg proposal."

Jasper sputtered. "I—I gave you what you've been asking for, didn't I? A proposal of marriage."

"That wasn't a proposal. It was a hatchet job!" Hazel roared.

Jasper scratched his head. "Didn't you see the ring? I spent a small fortune on it," Jasper shouted.

"Don't take this the wrong way, but you can take that piece of tin and give it to your next girlfriend. Consider yourself dumped, Mayor Prescott!" Hazel turned on her heel and stomped off toward the kitchen.

"Hazel!" Jasper began, walking after her.

Paige reached out and grabbed him by the arm. "I think you've done enough. I'll go after her."

Ruby jumped up from her seat. She looked at Liam. "I'm going to go check on Hazel. She didn't look so good." She shook her head at Jasper. "You should be ashamed of yourself."

Jasper threw up his hands and looked at Liam and Cameron. "What's wrong with everyone?"

Liam shook his head at his grandfather. "At the risk of asking a dumb question, are you crazy?"

"What? What just happened?" Jasper asked.

"What just happened?" Cameron roared. "Surely you can't be serious. You just hurt one of the most amazing, wonderful people in the world."

"Hazel shouldn't be hurt. She knows me. I'm not the sentimental sort. I'm not the type to get down on my knees and propose," Jasper muttered. The expression on his face showed that he was beginning to realize his huge misstep.

"Well, maybe just this once you should have done something to allow Hazel to live out her dream. It wouldn't have cost you anything, would it?" Liam pressed.

Jasper's face crumpled. "I…it's not my way. Hazel knows that."

"Really? Well, how's that working out for you right about now?" Cameron asked, his face a cold mask of fury.

Of all the Prescott siblings, Cameron shared the closest relationship with Hazel. She was his surrogate mother, employee and close friend. He was very protective of her.

As the band came back from their break and the intermission ended, Cameron left so he could resume his work duties. After a few minutes of sulking, Jasper got up and left the establishment. His shoulders were slumped, and he looked beaten. Liam couldn't help but feel a little badly for his grandfather. He suffered from a sort of blindness that wouldn't allow him to see his own faults and flaws. The way he had treated Hazel was shameless. And he didn't even seem to grasp what he had done wrong.

Liam felt a chill sweep over him as he realized something huge. He didn't want to be anything like Jasper. His grandfather was digging in his heels and refusing to acknowledge how wrong he had been. But what did his pride get him? He had lost Hazel and, from what Liam had seen, he would have an uphill battle getting her back.

Had he been walking in his own blindness? Refusing to even consider that Ruby's career was a calling rather than a threat to his family's stability? Protecting his heart rather than doing the brave thing—opening himself up to love. Putting oneself out there wasn't easy and it didn't feel totally comfortable, but Liam knew that Ruby was worth all the risks.

In the aftermath of her date night with Liam, Ruby found herself settling more and more into family life at the Prescott household. Things between her and Liam were good. More and more, she was imagining a permanent place for herself here in Love. With Liam and Aidan. With each passing day, Denver became nothing more than a blip on her radar. It was shocking how quickly she had shed her life in Colorado. And with each and every day, returning to Denver seemed less and less appealing.

Christmas was rapidly approaching. Ruby was getting really good at hiding presents all over the house. Some of her hiding places were so good she was beginning to fret that she might never find them. She had discussed with Liam the idea of buying Aidan a puppy for Christmas. Rita's litter hadn't been born yet, and they would need to stay with their mother for a few weeks after delivery. Aidan wanted a puppy so much, and since Liam was in agreement, Ruby wanted to make her son's dream come true.

Last night they had stayed in as a family and decorated the Christmas tree. Liam had brought her to tears by pulling out a box of antique ornaments that had been in her family for generations. Ruby had lovingly fingered them, admiring the stunning detail and the intricate craftsmanship. It made her sad that neither of her parents was alive to see Aidan or to help her navigate through life. No matter how old you were, there was always a yearning for a mother. She was no different. And she did have memories of the woman who had been her best friend and motivator. Most of her recollections were sketchy, but she had memories of a round-faced, cheerful woman who had loved to bake and shower her children with affection. Ruby could almost feel the tightness of her mother's hugs.

Her mother had passed on to her a love of the Christmas season. And now Ruby wanted to do something to pass on her family's legacy so that Aidan could know his heritage. That's where Kyle could be a big help. She was going to call him later today and invite him to Love for Christmas. Seeing how close Liam was to his siblings made her ache inside to strengthen her ties to her brother. And he could act as her living memory about their family traditions until those memories came back to her. Now, more than ever, she was optimistic about the bulk of her memories returning.

At the moment Ruby was sitting on the living room floor in front of the beautifully decorated tree, wrapping presents. Liam was right next to her, struggling with a tape dispenser and a roll of wrapping paper.

"Is there a secret to this?" Liam held up his hands. They were covered in tape.

Ruby chuckled and reached over to untangle him. "I take it that I used to do most of the wrapping?"

"Pretty much," Liam acknowledged. "Not that I didn't try, mind you, but you were way more talented at it than I was."

"It's okay. The true gift lies in the giving." She winked at Liam. "You've still got a shot at winning in that area."

Liam folded the wrapping paper and stuck the tape down. He held up the box. "It may not be the prettiest gift under the tree, but I stuck to it and I did it."

Ruby clapped. "Nicely done, Liam."

"I wanted to share something with you… My family has a Christmas tradition of going caroling a few days before Christmas. You used to love it. We go door to door, singing all types of Christmas songs."

"That's a great idea," Ruby said. "I imagine it's a real treat for the people whose houses you stop by. There's such joy in song."

"We're thinking of going tomorrow night. Are you okay with that? I don't want you to feel overwhelmed. The Prescotts can be a little wild and crazy during the holidays."

"Only during the holidays?" she teased. "Having just witnessed your grandfather's over-the-top proposal to Hazel, I'm going to hazard a guess that it's not just during the Christmas season."

Liam made a face. "Okay. I take that back. It's pretty much year-round with my family."

"The caroling sounds fun. Now that more of my memories have come back to me, I feel more comfortable being around groups of people. I don't feel like I'm stumbling around in the dark without a flashlight anymore."

"And you're developing friendships with Paige and Grace and Hazel. And Honor thinks you hung the moon. You're not an island anymore."

"You're right," Ruby said. "It helps to have connections here in town. I really enjoyed the tea party. And having Honor invite us out to the Wildlife Center. Those ladies are all something else," she said. "Grace is so adorable. And Hazel—" She let out a laugh. "She's a character if I've ever met one. And Paige… I don't know how or why, but she already seems like a close friend."

"Trust me. Those women can be a real lifeline here in this town. Each of them in their own way is made of strong stuff."

It was nice to hear Liam speak so well of Hazel, Honor and both his sisters-in-law. She thought very highly of all of them. And she looked forward to making those connections with Annie and Sophie, as well. That was the beauty of community. She hadn't experienced it in Colorado, but right here in Love, it was as natural as breathing. It was enmeshed in the fabric of the town.

"So, I don't want to bring up a tricky subject, but we never talked about your dad. Is he still in town?"

"Not that I know of," Liam said. "I grilled Jasper about it, but he said Pops never swung by his house. Can't say that I'm surprised."

"How's Jasper doing? Hazel seems to be staying firm in her resolve to be done with the relationship."

"He's in a little bit of a tailspin at the moment. At first he was in denial, but now the anger is coming out. I'm hoping he just fast-forwards to the acceptance part."

Ruby made a tutting sound. "I feel kind of sorry for him."

"What? Why? He broke Hazel's heart," Liam said.

"Yeah, but I think his heart must be a little roughed up, too. I think Jasper pretends not to care as much as he really does care deep down. Get it?" Ruby asked.

"I see what you're saying, but at this point in his life he needs to get his act together. Tomorrow isn't promised to anyone. We all need to own up to our truths." Liam looked over at her. He seemed slightly preoccupied about something, but he didn't seem inclined to share it with her.

She threw her tape down on to the carpet and turned to Liam. "I have an idea!"

Liam's mouth twisted. "Should I be worried?"

"No. It's brilliant. Why don't we play matchmaker for them? Hazel and Jasper! Think about it. Jasper is the one who created the Operation Love program. He's brought dozens of women to this town and helped Alaskan bachelors find love. Your brother met his wife through the program. So did Declan! Shouldn't we try and give something back to Jasper?"

Liam let out a sigh. "When you put it like that, I guess we do owe Jasper a little consideration. What exactly did you have in mind?"

It was a perfect Alaskan winter night for caroling. The temperature was a chilly fifteen degrees Fahrenheit. Snow was lightly falling as they headed out on foot from the center of town. With a full moon hanging high in the sky and the heavens lit up with sparkling stars, their path was made clear for them. There couldn't be a more perfect December night.

It was a full crew for caroling, but it truly did feel like the more the merrier. Liam had surprised her by inviting Kyle to come and join them. Jasper, Hazel, Boone, Grace, Cameron and Paige were also there. Jasper and Hazel were avoiding each other like the plague. Emma had stayed at home with her nanny, Fiona, since she had just recovered from her ear infection, and neither Paige nor Cameron wanted to run the risk of a relapse. Honor was there, as well as Sophie, Declan and Annie. And Pastor Jack Teagan, who made a point of telling Ruby he'd been the one to officiate her wedding.

Ruby was happy to see everyone. And she no longer felt like a stranger among the townsfolk or with Liam's family. She was part of them now. A citizen of this quirky Alaskan town. A Prescott.

They went door to door, singing beloved Christmas songs. More times than not they were invited inside for holiday treats and hot cocoa. Some townsfolk handed them candy canes or put their coats on and joined them in the revelry. Ruby couldn't think of a more festive way to spend an evening. And to make it even more special, she had a flash of being heavily pregnant with Aidan and going door to door, her hand firmly clasped in Liam's.

"I think that's it for the hot chocolate, Aidan," Ruby said. "You're going to end up with a bellyache."

"But, Mom, I don't feel sick at all," Aidan protested, his little mouth turned down in a frown.

Ruby stopped in her tracks, blown away by hearing Aidan call her "Mom." He continued to walk ahead with the group, totally unaware of what had just happened or how it had impacted her. Liam stopped and stood by her side. A smile threatened to take over his face. He looked almost as happy as she felt.

"Did you just hear that?" she whispered. "Or did I imagine it?"

"I heard it. I don't need to ask you how it feels to hear him say that one very special word. It's written all over your face."

Tears pooled in her eyes. She began to sniff to keep them at bay. "I can't even put it into words. I feel like I could soar right now."

Liam reached out for her mittened hand and squeezed it. They began walking toward the group of carolers, hand in hand. For the first time in forever, Ruby felt like part of a couple. And it felt wonderful to know she wasn't alone in the world. She was tied to something so much bigger than herself. There wasn't any other place she'd rather be at this moment than right at Liam's side.

"Why don't we invite everyone over to the house for a small gathering? We were already planning to have people over. What's a few more?" Ruby suggested. The expression on her face was one of pure excitement. Her cheeks were pink from the cold, and he could tell from the way she was jamming her hands into her coat pockets that she was trying to stay warm.

"Everyone? Are you sure?" he asked, filled with surprise at Ruby's willingness to host a large gathering. It was a generous suggestion, particularly since she was still getting used to being around large groups of people.

"What about the plan for Jasper and Hazel? I'm not sure Jasper wants more of an audience for his big moment."

"Yes, I'm sure about including everyone. We have enough food to feed a small army, and Aidan will love having a house full of guests. Plus, it will make things more romantic when Jasper's plan comes to fruition. He owes Hazel big-time after the last one."

Liam hoped Ruby wasn't disappointed. His grandfather was a feisty, opinionated man who tended to dig his heels in when he wanted to be ornery. There was never a guarantee with Jasper that he would follow along with anything, even a plan that might reunite him with Hazel and put him back in her good graces.

As they stood on Jarvis Street, Liam put his hands together and let out a whistle to gain everyone's attention. The group quieted and shifted their attention to him. "Ruby, Aidan and I would like to invite everyone back to our place for a light meal, fellowship and holiday cheer."

Judging by the reaction, everyone was excited about attending a gathering at their home. There was clapping and cheering from the group. Jasper let out a groan and made a face at him. He didn't think he'd ever seen his grandfather so nervous and agitated. He prayed this didn't mean he was about to bail on the plan. Aidan was doing a little dance in the snow and sticking his tongue out so that he could taste the snowflakes. He dove into the snow then picked up a handful, lifting in the air and lobbying it in his father's direction.

Plop. It landed on Liam's shoulder. With a wild roar he raced toward his son, who let out a shriek and began running in the other direction. Before long, snowballs were being lobbed in all directions by everyone. Liam couldn't remember the last time he'd had this much fun. Joy pulsed sure and strong in the air. The spirit of the season could be felt right there on Jarvis Street among this group of townsfolk.

Once they arrived at the house, Liam opened the doors and let everyone in. He grabbed Ruby by the hand and pulled her back outside.

"What's going on? Aren't we supposed to be inside?" she asked with a laugh. "Jasper looks like he's about to jump out of his skin. You might need to settle him down so this can go off without a hitch."

"Jasper will be fine. I just wanted you to see something."

He pulled her into the yard so that they were facing their big bay window. "Look." He pointed up at the window.

Ruby let out a gasp of pure awe. "Liam. It's magnificent."

Liam and Ruby stood for a moment and simply admired the way their Christmas tree looked from outside. The lights shimmered and winked at them, dazzling in their beauty. The gold star glinted from on top of the tree. Their home looked warm and festive and inviting. In his heart of hearts, Liam had never imagined Christmas could ever feel this heartwarming ever again. It was true that a house wasn't a home. Ruby being back meant all the difference in their world.

She had brought so much along with her—hope, joy, heart. And he knew now that her return also served to provide him with a second chance to get things right. Part of doing that would be facing down his fears and telling Ruby the truth about their marriage problems. He simply couldn't exist in all this beauty while sitting on something so big. It was the only way he could save their relationship from future bumps and bruises. If they were going to have an open and honest relationship, he was going to have to be transparent.

"It's simply beautiful, Liam." Ruby let out a sigh. "This whole evening has been so joyful. Being with family and friends. Seeing Aidan so happy. The caroling door to door."

Liam grinned with pleasure. "It was a night to remember, that's for sure."

"I felt like a kid again singing like that. I was in the

choir, you know," she boasted. Yet another thing she felt blessed to have remembered.

"It's a good thing you're easy on the eyes because your singing voice needs some work," Liam teased. Her singing voice had always been something he'd been able to tease her about.

Ruby swatted him with her mitten. "Hey! That's not very nice."

Liam was laughing so hard he clutched his stomach. "Maybe not, but it's true."

"I'm very insulted," she said in a prim voice.

"I'm sorry. It's just that you're amazing at everything under the sun. That's the only thing I could ever tease you about," Liam admitted.

"It's not the sound of the voice that's important. It's the way you put your heart and soul into it," Ruby said, trying not to chuckle.

All of a sudden Liam stopped laughing. Her words represented way more to him than she realized. It signified the way he wanted to walk in the world. Heart. Soul. Truth. He couldn't imagine being wrong when being led by those values.

"You're right about that, Ruby. And no one sang tonight with more heart than you did. You radiate from inside."

"I'm happy. I think that explains it," she said in a soft voice.

Happiness. It wasn't a concept he'd allowed himself to think about for some time. Not since his entire world had fallen apart in the wake of Ruby's "death." His feelings for Ruby were more powerful than he could put into words. He had always loved her, but now he was falling in love with her all over again. Step by step, moment by moment, she was making indelible impressions on his heart. And the sheer power of it scared him to death.

"You're a beautiful woman, Ruby Prescott. Inside and out." Liam reached out and ran his palm across her cheek.

He lowered his head and captured her lips in a stunning kiss that took her breath away. Her legs almost gave way beneath her. It felt as if she was being swept away. Despite the frosty cold, Liam's lips were warm and inviting as they moved against hers. Ruby reached up and grabbed the fabric of his coat, pulling him closer. She wrapped her arms around his neck, anchoring herself to him. Ruby wanted to show him that she was in this—with every fiber of her being she wanted to be Mrs. Liam Prescott. She wanted him! And Aidan. And a life filled with all the blessings that had been on full display tonight.

As the kiss ended, she found herself standing on wobbly legs. With a grin, Liam steadied her by holding her arms. Who would have thought a simple kiss would feel so earth-shattering? The attraction between them was electric. It even managed to cut through the chill in the frosty night air.

"Let's head inside. We need to give those two lovebirds a push in the right direction," Ruby whispered.

"Just don't be too disappointed if it doesn't work out the way you plan," Liam warned. "As a Prescott, I've learned to expect the unexpected."

"Have a little faith," she said as they walked inside.

After taking off her winter parka, Ruby made her way into the kitchen, pleased that everyone was helping themselves to food and drinks. Prior to leaving for the caroling outing Ruby had laid out most of the food on the dining room table. Although they had only planned on a small number of guests, Ruby felt grateful they had enough food to accommodate a larger number of people. She busied herself filling up the punch bowl with eggnog and taking the shrimp and deli platters out of the fridge and placing them on the table. Honor had set up all the desserts on the side table. At the moment Aidan and a few of his little friends were helping themselves to cookies and brownies.

All of a sudden Jasper appeared at her side. He tugged at her arm. "Ruby, I need to talk to you in private."

"Now?" she asked with a frown. "Is this about you-know-what?"

"If you-know-what involves the diamond ring sitting in my pocket…then, yes," he responded with a loud whisper. "I'm about to burst."

Ruby quickly led him to the office at the back of the house that Liam used when he worked from home. Once they were alone and she had closed the door behind them, Jasper began to vent.

"I'm not sure about this plan anymore. Seems to me that I would be groveling. Jasper Prescott doesn't beg."

"Jasper, this isn't about your pride. It's about repairing the damage you did the other night. That went down in a public arena, so it's only fitting that you reverse things in the same way."

His lips trembled. "But what if she says no, Ruby? I'm not sure this old heart of mine could take the rejection again."

Sympathy flared inside her. At his heart Jasper wasn't quite the curmudgeon he appeared to be. He was a man who hid a lot of his feelings behind a façade of irreverence. It was a mechanism he had most likely developed after the death of his first wife and the heartache he had suffered as a result of that huge loss. After all, it took a man with a mighty big heart to conceive of the Operation Love program.

"I'm not going to lie to you and say that it's not possible, Jasper. But how will you ever know if you don't try?" She reached out and squeezed his hand. He was trembling. "I know what it feels like to be afraid. I've been dealing with fear for the last two years. One of the bravest things I've ever done is get on that seaplane—destination Love, Alaska. And the second will be laying my heart wide open for Liam to claim it. Am I afraid that he won't? Of course. But I can't let that stop me. God led me home for a purpose. And I can't run from that, even if it terrifies me at times."

Jasper reached up and cupped her face between his palms. "You belong to us, Ruby. You're a Prescott through and through, but you're also a big part of this town. Love needs your big heart and your courage. I feel blessed to call you my granddaughter."

Jasper pulled her into his arms. Ruby blinked away tears as she sank into the hug. Deep down, Jasper was a cuddly teddy bear. She loved this man, warts and all. And she wanted him to have his happy ending with Hazel.

"I think I'm going to need to borrow some of your courage," Jasper said in a raspy voice.

"You've got this, Jasper. Just speak from your heart and try to focus on what Hazel brings into your life."

"Hmm. Good things, right?" he asked with a frown.

"Jasper!" Ruby cried out, gently swatting him.

He threw his head back and laughed. "Just a little joke. I had to get it out of my system before I make my pitch."

Ruby studied him. "Are you ready?"

"As I'll ever be," he muttered as he wrenched the door open and strode back into the party.

Ruby trailed behind him, not wanting to miss his moment.

Jasper walked into the living room, where the majority of guests were gathered. He looked around the room and finally spotted Hazel sitting next to Grace on the couch. When she spotted him approaching, she gave him the stink-eye. She did it so well Ruby thought she could give lessons on it.

"Hazel! We need to talk," Jasper announced. Ruby made a face at Jasper. He was starting off on the wrong foot. He needed to be tender, not gruff.

"I don't need to do anything! We're no longer an item in case that addled brain of yours forgot!" Hazel said. She made a slashing motion in the air with her hand. "We're history! Kaput!"

Yikes! This was not going to be easy, Ruby feared.

She met Liam's eyes from where he was standing across the room. His expression was doubtful.

"I love you, Hazel Tookes!" Jasper shouted.

The room got extraordinarily quiet. All eyes were glued to the unfolding drama. Guests began to trickle in from the other rooms to watch.

Hazel's eyes widened. Ruby imagined she'd never heard Jasper declare his feelings in such a public forum. He moved closer and took Hazel's hand in his. "The other night I made a plum fool of myself. And in the process, I dragged you down with me. I'll regret that for the rest of my life.

"Hazel, you know that I already had the love of a lifetime."

Hazel nodded. "Yes. Your wife, Harmony."

Jasper nodded. "She was a fine woman. I lost her due to a mixture of my pig-headedness and her pride. I never imagined God would bless me twice in my life. But he did, Hazel. He brought me you. He sent me a supportive, beautiful woman who is my best friend. Someone I can laugh with and confide in, a woman who knows me inside and out, yet still thinks I'm worth loving. Half the time I know that I don't deserve you, Hazel. What you've brought me and the entire Prescott clan is beyond anything I can articulate with mere words."

By this time tears were streaming down Hazel's face and she was choking back sobs. Ruby felt moisture on her own cheeks. A quick look around the room showed that most were becoming emotional. The raw emotion emanating from Jasper was undeniable.

"Would you make this old fool the happiest man

in Alaska and consent to marry me?" He dug in his pocket for the ring box and popped it open. The diamond glinted and winked at Hazel from its throne. "I'd get down on one knee, but I'm not sure I would be able to get up."

The room broke into laughter. Ruby looked over at Liam. He seemed as if he might burst with pride. Hazel stood and wrapped her arms around Jasper's neck. She stared deeply into his eyes. "Jasper, you've made me the happiest woman in the world. All I ever wanted was to know that you loved me. And if you really want me as your bride, my answer is yes. A thousand times yes." She leaned in and placed a smooch on Jasper's lips that sealed the deal.

The room erupted into chaos. Shouts. Cheers. Whistles. The next thing Ruby knew Liam and Aidan were both at her side, sharing the heartwarming moment with her. Liam reached for her hand and squeezed it. It felt so right having their hands linked, as if they belonged together.

Ruby blinked back tears.

Jasper taking this leap of faith and putting his pride aside was a mighty thing indeed.

This had been a perfect evening, capped off by the knowledge that Jasper and Hazel had been blissfully reunited. Finally she could allow herself to believe in the possibility of a happily-ever-after with Liam. If someone as set in his ways as Jasper could make this huge shift, anything was possible. And she needed to believe, since she'd fallen in love all over again with her husband.

Hope shimmered in the room like the gold star on the Christmas tree.

Chapter Twelve

Ruby sat in the kitchen, studying one of her favorite cookbooks. She had volunteered to make the turkey for Christmas dinner at Jasper's house, and she had no intention of delivering a dry, pathetic excuse for a turkey. Nope. It wasn't happening. This turkey was going to go down in Love, Alaska, history as the juiciest, most succulent bird of all time. Liam would be so proud of her. And she would be extremely proud of herself, as well.

Something had been bothering her all morning. She had a slight headache and there was a strange feeling of dread hovering over her. It didn't make any sense, considering all that was right in her world. Aidan was now calling her Mom. Her memories were slowly but surely coming back to her. And her relationship with Liam had turned romantic. Last night's kiss had definitely moved them out of the friend zone. There was no doubt in her mind that she was falling in love with her husband.

Just the thought of it gave her goose bumps.

Meeting Liam for lunch at the Moose Café would serve as a nice treat in the middle of the day. And it felt much better to spend time with him than to sit around daydreaming about the tall, dark and handsome doctor who had captured her heart.

Aidan sat at a little table with Emma, who was hanging out with Cameron at work today. From what Ruby observed, the two kids did more playing than eating. It was nice to watch the two of them together. Although there was a three-year age difference, they got along like two peas in a pod.

Liam swung his gaze from Aidan to her. "Something tells me Aidan wants a little sister or brother someday. We always wanted a big family."

Ruby took a sip of her coffee. "We did?" she asked, her heart thundering inside her chest.

"At least ten," Liam drawled.

Ruby's jaw dropped. "Ten? Seriously?"

Liam's grin threatened to take over his entire face. "No, I'm teasing, but we did want more."

She looked over at Aidan and smiled. "He'd be a great big brother."

"It's obvious to me that you're feeling more settled now in Love," Liam said as he gulped down his coffee.

"I am," Ruby said. "There were a few bumps on the road. It was hard for me to know what the future held for me without my memories. But that's changed quite a bit. A lot of my memories have trickled back. I feel more grounded now."

"I admire you," Liam said. "When you first arrived

in Love, your head must have been spinning. You really held on to your faith."

"I have no doubt that God sent me here. Imagine if I hadn't come seeking answers." She shuddered. "You and Aidan might never have known that I survived the accident." The thought of it was terrifying. Her whole life would have been different. It was painful to even think about not reuniting with Liam and Aidan.

Liam reached for her hand and raised it to his lips. "I will always be grateful for God pointing you in the direction of home."

"Me, too," Ruby murmured, overwhelmed by the magnitude of how much her life had changed in the past few weeks. Before coming to Love she had been pretty much a loner, one who wasn't tied to anything or anyone. Now, she had a family, one she loved with all her heart. And her future was ripe with promise.

After lunch ended, Ruby took Aidan to the library to pick up a few books. He was at the age when he needed to get started on the road to reading. Next fall he would be headed to kindergarten.

Annie greeted them as soon as they walked inside. With her sweet nature and extensive knowledge of the library's catalog, Annie made their visit engaging and wonderful. They ended up with both of their arms full of books by the time they departed.

When they finally arrived home, it was Aidan's nap time.

Ruby stuffed her library books into a shopping bag she had tucked away in the trunk. She placed the strap of the bag over her shoulder and prepared to help Aidan lug their finds inside.

"Hi, Ruby. Aidan." Gareth was on the porch, sitting in one of the Adirondack chairs. He stood as they came closer.

Aidan reached for her hand and warily studied his grandfather.

"Do you remember me?" Gareth asked, bending over until he was at Aidan's eye level.

Aidan shrugged and looked up at Ruby. He turned to Gareth and said, "Not really, but I've seen pictures of you from when my daddy was little."

Gareth winced. "I'm sorry I haven't been around more often, A-man. It's great to see you, buddy."

Ruby frowned at her father-in-law. "What are you doing here, Gareth? Liam thought you left Love."

His smile twisted. "I was visiting some friends in Homer. But I didn't get very far before I realized that I needed to come back and talk to my children."

"Liam is at the clinic." She frowned at him. "But I'm sure you know that already."

He had a sheepish expression on his face. "I'd like to have a few minutes to talk to you, Ruby. To apologize. To explain myself."

"Come on in, Gareth." Once they crossed the threshold, she turned to him and whispered, "I'm only extending this courtesy to you since you're Liam's father. A bit ironic, I'd say, considering you haven't given any of your kids much of that."

Turning toward her son, Ruby said, "Aidan, you need to go take your nap. You're about to crash."

"But I don't want to go to sleep," he complained. The way his lids had been slowly creeping closed had showed he was fighting sleep.

"Listen to your mother, kiddo. I promise we'll do something fun together really soon." He stuck out his hand. Aidan grinned and shook it, then retreated to his room.

"Come on into the kitchen," Ruby said, leading the way. She took down two glasses and filled them with lemonade. Gareth sat across from her at the table.

For a moment he looked down, avoiding her gaze. "I was your mentor, so I feel a little bit of responsibility to keep tabs on you. I know that might sound strange to you, considering how I've dropped the ball with my own kids."

Anger on Liam's behalf rose inside her. "You did more than drop the ball. Your vanishing acts have really hurt your children. That's unacceptable."

Gareth looked up at her. His eyes were full of shame. "I know. I'm determined to change all that moving forward. I really want to try." He reached for his glass and took a sip of lemonade.

Ruby nodded. "I respect that."

"If you have even the slightest inclination to return to search and rescue, I'm here to answer any questions. And I know that might place me in the crosshairs of my son, but this isn't personal. It's professional. I was the one who called you in for that Colorado mission." His face blanched. "I feel responsible for everything that happened."

Ruby shrugged. "You shouldn't feel that way. Life

happens. And with regard to my career, I'm just going to have to wait and see. It's too soon to know anything."

"I can appreciate that. You've been through a lot, Ruby. I'm really happy that you and Liam got past all of your marital problems."

Her heart constricted. She frowned at him. "Problems? What are you talking about?"

Gareth's face fell. His mouth opened then quickly closed.

"What problems?" she persisted. The pounding inside her chest was getting louder by the second.

He held up his hands as if to ward her off. "Ruby, please. I didn't come here to make trouble."

"Tell me, Gareth." She wasn't taking no for an answer.

He let out a sigh and shook his head. "You were struggling with a few marriage issues. It would have blown over. I know it."

Marriage issues? Hadn't everyone said that she had enjoyed a perfect marriage? If something had been wrong in their marriage, Liam would have told her. He was a straight shooter, not the type to harbor secrets.

"I've said enough!" Gareth said in a fierce voice. "It's all in the past. Liam will never forgive me for opening this can of worms." With a tortured groan, Gareth rose jerkily from the table and pushed his chair in. "I really did come here today to make inroads." He strode from the room, quickly making his way to the front door.

"Gareth!" she called after him. Without turning back to her, he wrenched open the front door and disappeared from view.

Once she opened the front door Gareth was already in his car, taking off down the road. She closed the door and sagged against it, filled with confusion about Gareth's revelation. She didn't necessarily take Gareth at face value, but she was of the mind that his comment had been truthful. The immediate look of regret on his face once he had realized his mistake had been authentic.

She began to tremble. Gareth had been telling her the truth. She knew it instinctively. This was the thing she had been so afraid to discover. This was the monster hiding under the bed. And she had been so afraid to remember it because on some level she knew it might change everything between her and Liam.

Ruby began to knead her head with her fingers. Her head ached. She sat on the couch and wrapped her arms around her middle. She began rocking slightly back and forth.

Suddenly she had a flash of the fight with Liam. His face had been a cold mask of anger. She had been crying and speaking in a raised voice. As if she was watching a movie, she heard herself ask for a separation. She saw the hurt look etched on Liam's face followed by his blistering anger.

It had been about her job! The words "dangerous" and "Aidan" and "mission" had been flowing in the conversation. She had wrenched her rings off and placed them in a red-velvet box in his dresser drawer. There had been tears and raised voices between her and Liam. Then resignation as she calmly began packing her duffel bag.

It made sense. For so long she had wondered about where her wedding rings were and what had happened to them. She had never asked Liam about it, nor had he given her the rings back. That in itself was a red flag. Wouldn't Liam have mentioned her wedding rings? Unless, of course, he hadn't wanted to bring them up, knowing she had made the decision not to wear the rings shortly before the accident.

Dear Lord. Please let this be a false memory. Please don't let this be real. I want so badly to believe in Liam...to believe in us and our marriage. I don't know how I can do that if Liam hasn't been honest with me.

Filled with determination, Ruby took a deep breath and headed down the hall to the master bedroom. She slowly turned the knob and stepped inside. Goose bumps popped up on her arms. This was the scene she remembered from her flash. She looked toward the twin dressers standing side by side. It wasn't right to go through Liam's private belongings, but she had to know if what she remembered had really happened.

She pulled open the top dresser drawer. There were a few items inside…mainly socks. In the corner sat a crimson box. Taking it out, she lifted it open with shaking fingers. Inside were two rings—a solitaire diamond and a wedding band with a row of smaller diamond stones.

Ruby let out a small cry. She felt as if someone had just placed a twenty-pound weight on her chest. It was difficult to breathe. All she wanted to do at the moment was to curl up on the floor and sob.

Footsteps sounded behind her on the hardwood floor. Startled, she whirled around. Liam was standing there, a look of unease stamped on his face.

"I couldn't bear to tell you. I tried several times, but I never could do it." His voice sounded ragged.

"You didn't try hard enough," she cried. "All of this time you could have said something to me. You had plenty of moments."

He took a step toward her. She held up her hands to ward him off. She needed to keep him at a distance.

"You were trying to get your life back and bond with our son. Flashes of memory were returning to you. Maybe it was selfish, but I didn't want to run the risk of everything falling apart if you found out."

"I took off my wedding rings. We were breaking up. That's huge." She felt numb. How she had prayed this one memory wasn't true. But it was true, and now she had to figure out what it meant for her marriage to Liam.

He nodded. "It's true that we weren't in a good place, Ruby."

His admission frightened her. Suddenly every ounce of security she had established in Love felt as if it were slipping out of her grasp. She raised her hand to her mouth as a sob bubbled up inside her. Why had he allowed her to believe they were a storybook couple?

"I can't believe this! Everything I believed about us is a lie."

"No! It wasn't a lie. Relationships ebb and flow, Ruby. Sure, we were grappling with certain issues, but we loved each other. That's the biggest truth of all."

"But we were separating. Breaking up," she cried out.

"We would have found our way back to one another. I know it!"

She sank onto the bed as if her legs were too weak

to hold her up. "It feels like I don't know much of anything. Everything between us since I've been back in Love has been based on what I thought we had. Everyone here in town told me we were this amazing couple, but the truth is, they didn't know our struggles or that we might not have stayed together."

"I know this is confusing to you, but it doesn't change what we were…the love we shared. We were devoted to each other, Ruby. Head-over-heels, besotted, crazy-in-love fools. Did we have rough times? Yes. Did we fall short of what we wanted to be? Yes. But the good times far outweighed the bad." A sheen of tears shone in his eyes. "I know we would have stuck it out because I vowed it to you on the day we got married."

She shook her head. "If all that is true, why weren't you honest with me?"

"Because after losing you, I couldn't stand the thought of going through it all over again. I wasn't confident that I could tell you without losing you. I allowed fear to cloud my better judgment. I was afraid for Aidan, as well, and what it would mean for him if you took off back to Colorado."

"Stop hiding behind Aidan! Ever since I came back you've been avoiding the elephant in the room. You made me believe that we had this beautiful, perfect marriage. And so did everyone else in this town—" Suddenly she wasn't just furious with Liam. She was angry at the townsfolk for giving credence to the fairy tale. And she was furious with God, for allowing her to believe she had found her way back to the place she belonged.

"It wasn't perfect, but it was everything we ever wanted it to be."

"That's not true," she said in a steely voice. "I remember the fighting and the bitterness. We were planning a separation. That's not what most couples dream about."

Liam grimaced. "You brought up the idea of a separation after things got heated between us. I hated the fact that you were going out on these dangerous missions and putting your life at risk. One of your search-and-rescue colleagues had been killed in a previous mission. I wanted you here in Love, with us, where it was safe."

Ruby raised her hand to her head. It still ached. "And I told you that my profession was a big part of me and that I wouldn't be whole without it."

Liam nodded, his expression grim. "Neither of us was willing to budge."

"So we broke?" Ruby's lips quivered. She had bought into the fairy tale of her blissful marriage to Liam. The perfect couple with the high-powered careers and the adorable son. Not a single person had described them as anything other than euphoric. Suddenly nothing made sense. Liam wasn't the man or the partner she had believed him to be. And it hurt terribly. The pain threatened to strangle her.

"We weren't broken. A little chipped and frayed around the edges, perhaps. But none of that is what's most important. We're two people who were given an opportunity to repair the pain in our marriage. Try to remember us, Ruby. Who we truly were. What we can be again."

She shook her head. "Nothing beautiful or lasting

can be built on deception. I remember enough to know that, Liam. It wasn't pretty."

"I think you're falling in love with me all over again. You already have my heart, Ruby. There's nothing standing in our way. Let's not put up obstacles."

She gathered her strength and stood. "So, tell me one thing, Liam. Would you still hold me back from doing search-and-rescue work?"

"Don't ask me that question." Liam gritted his teeth.

She locked gazes with him, letting him know in no uncertain terms that she expected an answer.

He let out a groan. "My head says no, but my heart says yes. I lost you once due to unacceptable risks. How could I ever be on board with you returning to that line of work?" His brow was furrowed. His features radiated intensity.

Ruby shuddered. Up until today it had felt as if they were moving toward their own happily-ever-after. But now, after what she had discovered, it felt as if everything was falling apart.

"I need to go, Liam. I can't keep going around and around this with you. Aidan is taking his nap." She began walking toward the door. Liam reached out and grabbed her arm. She shrugged him off.

"Please don't go. Stay and talk this through with me. There's not a thing we can't figure out together." There was a pleading quality to Liam's voice that made her want to stick around and hash things out. But she was so confused about everything. At the moment she didn't know up from down. And she needed time to sort things through.

"I can't. Truthfully, it's really hard for me to look at you right now."

She raced to the living room, picked up her purse and keys and headed out into the Alaskan afternoon. Ruby had no idea where she was headed, but the one thing she knew for certain was that she no longer felt safe and secure in her world.

Liam watched through the bay window as Ruby roared off down the road. Pain ricocheted through him like bullets. He closed his eyes and prayed to God for a reprieve. This was what he had been so afraid of—losing Ruby all over again. It was the reason he had steeled his heart from her until she had worn down his defenses. Once again, he felt like he was being ripped up inside. And there was nothing he could do to stop the tidal wave of pain. He just had to endure it.

He had failed Aidan. And Ruby. And, ultimately, himself.

"Daddy?" Liam turned at the sound of Aidan's sleep-infused voice.

"Hey, A-man," he said. He was trying his best to keep his voice normal. The last thing he wanted was to upset Aidan. "How was your nap?"

"I had a bad dream. There was a snow monster and it came to take Mommy." His lips trembled and he raised his arms to be lifted up.

Liam scooped Aidan into his arms and patted his back to soothe him. "Aw, I'm sorry. Nightmares can be really scary. They seem so real, don't they?"

Aidan nodded as he wiped away tears with the back of his hand. "Where's Mommy?"

"She had to go out for a little bit."

Aidan frowned. "But what if something happened to her? What if the snow monster got her again?"

Liam walked over to the couch and set Aidan down. He sat next to him. "She didn't get eaten by the snow monster. That's not going to happen again."

"Promise?"

"Yes. I can't promise that nothing bad is ever going to happen, but I can tell you for sure that the snow monster isn't going to hurt your mother. Not ever again."

Aidan nestled his head against Liam's chest. He felt his heart tighten painfully. The love he felt for his son knew no bounds. It literally threatened to bring him to his knees. And it terrified him to think his actions had jeopardized their family's future. Because of him and the pressures he'd placed on her, Ruby might choose not to stick around.

Please, Lord. Don't let Ruby walk away from us. She's the love of my life. The mother of my child. Give me an opportunity to make things right and to show her that there's nothing we can't get past.

Ruby drove around Love with her thoughts jumbled and chaotic. She had no idea of where to go. Every tie she had in this town led straight back to Liam. Liam. The man she loved. It was too late to rein herself in. She had already fallen deeply, completely, in love with him. And now, knowing their marriage had been in trouble, she had no clue what it meant for their future.

Did they even have one now? Liam hadn't been honest with her. How could their future be built on a lie? She didn't know if she could trust him moving forward. She felt almost as confused as she had when she'd first arrived in town.

After riding around for a while, Ruby parked her car in front of the Love Free Library. It was such a beautiful place. Maybe she could go in and sit somewhere soothing so she could think. Annie seemed to be the sort of person who wouldn't pry and, if she needed to, she would be someone to confide in about Liam.

Ruby walked toward the library and looked up at the gold-and-cream library sign. She stopped to read the words etched on the front of the library. *Love is patient. Love is kind.* The verse from Corinthians. She knew it on a deep level. It spoke to her.

Liam had recited it to her at their wedding. It had been part of their vows. And she had recited it to him, as well. She could see it all in her mind's eye. Her romantic, elegant wedding gown. Liam looking handsome in his dark tux with his brothers at his side. In her hand she'd held a bouquet of forget-me-nots as she walked down the aisle on Kyle's arm. There had been such a look of love stamped on Liam's face as Pastor Jack pronounced them husband and wife.

More than anything, she recalled the way she had felt that day. Hopeful. Certain. Committed. She had known on that day that she had wanted to be married to Liam Prescott more than anything else in the world.

Ruby quickly reversed herself and headed straight back to the car. At this moment all she felt was overwhelming love and gratitude for the man she had vowed to love for a lifetime.

* * *

Liam heard the front door open with a bang. Ruby! He walked toward the hallway. Ruby was standing in the foyer. He stopped, uncertain as to what he was walking toward.

"Liam!" With a wild cry, Ruby dropped her purse and beat a fast path toward him. He met her halfway, reaching down and gathering her up by her waist so that she was in his arms.

He was cradling her against him, not wanting to ever let her go. Although he'd known it wasn't likely, he'd feared that she might never come back to him. The very thought of it had been unbearable.

He set her down, gazing into her tear-filled brown eyes. "I'm so happy you're back. I love you so much."

"Oh, Liam, I never should have walked out. I should have stuck around to listen and try to understand."

He smoothed her hair back and kissed her on her forehead. "Shh. I don't care. What's important is that you're here. And I plan to show you how much I love you, Ruby. You'll never have to doubt us ever again."

Tears streamed down Ruby's face. "No, I won't ever question it again. I love you, Liam. After I left here, God pointed me in the right direction. He shined a bright light on our love. I remembered our wedding day and the vows we exchanged. Love is patient. Love is kind."

Liam blinked past his own tears. "Love never fails."

"Love never fails," Ruby repeated, reaching up on her tiptoes to place a tender kiss on her husband's lips.

"I'm going to support you, Ruby, no matter what decisions you make in the future about your career. There's no way anything is going to tear us apart. After everything we've been through, the rest should be a cakewalk."

"What matters is that we're in this for the long haul. That's what we promised each other on our wedding day. That we would stick it out come what may." Tears pooled in Ruby's eyes. She was getting choked up. "I promise never to forget the road that led us to where we are today."

"Marry me, Ruby." He cupped her face between his palms.

"Did you forget? We're already married," Ruby said with a chuckle.

"In some ways that was a lifetime ago. Let's renew our vows. At Christmas. Let's remind all our friends and family that our love has endured...and is thriving. Let's serve as an example that love is worth fighting for."

"I'll marry you again, Dr. Prescott. Today. Tomorrow. Any day of the week."

Liam dipped his head and placed a triumphant kiss on his wife's lips. He hoped it conveyed everything he felt for her and all the hopes he held for their future.

"I'm going to hold you to that, my beautiful Ruby."

The lights from the Christmas tree sparkled brightly as Liam and Ruby kissed to celebrate their happy news. Years ago at Christmas they had committed themselves to walking through life together. Now, all these years later, they were going to do it all over again. Ruby and Liam knew the most important thing of all was to love one another.

Epilogue

"So what's my job again?" Aidan asked as he looked up at his father.

Liam and Aidan had just finished changing into their tuxedoes in one of the waiting rooms inside the church. Liam bent down to fix Aidan's crimson bow tie so it would sit straight instead of crooked.

"Your job is to stand up for me as my best man," Liam said. He reached out and tousled his son's curly hair. "You have to hand me the rings when it's time to put them on Mommy's finger."

Aidan grinned, showcasing a missing front tooth. He had lost his very first tooth two nights ago and had been showing it off ever since. "She's going to be happy about the new stone you added. It's awesome."

Liam took the ring out of his pocket and admired it for a moment. The ruby stone sparkled next to the diamonds. It signified a new beginning. The past had been their foundation, but they were looking forward to a future ripe with promise. Over the last few weeks they had both learned what mattered most. Above all else, their family reigned supreme. And despite any obstacles that might come their way, they were in this for life. *Till death do us part.*

"I'll hold on to these until we get to the altar," Liam suggested, tucking the rings into his jacket pocket.

"Phew," Aidan said, wiping his hand across his forehead. "That's a lot of responsibility for a kid."

A slight tapping noise drew their attention to the door.

"Come in," Liam called out, wondering if Pastor Jack or one of his brothers had stopped by to check in. The door slowly opened to reveal Ruby standing at the threshold in her ivory wedding gown.

For a moment all Liam could do was gape at her. Her long hair had been swept up in an elegant twist, with tendrils of hair framing her beautiful face. The dress—the same one she'd worn at their original wedding—was romantic and ethereal. A crown of holly and red berries sat on top of her head, serving as a glorious reminder of their Christmas wedding.

Liam couldn't form a sentence for a few seconds. The sight of his bride in her full wedding regalia was mind-blowing. "Ruby, you look…magnificent."

"Mom, you look so pretty." Aidan chimed in.

"Thank you," Ruby said. She winked at Aidan. "Both of you look incredibly handsome. You sure clean up well."

Aidan frowned at her. He looked back and forth between his parents. "Hey! I thought the two of you weren't supposed to see each other before the ceremony."

"Technically, that is the tradition…" Ruby hedged.

"But since we're already married, I don't think we're breaking any rules."

Aidan shrugged. "Sounds good to me."

"Hey, buddy, why don't you go see if Jasper is here? I think your mom might want to tell me something in private," Liam said.

"Sure thing," Aidan said. "I'll be right back. I'm going to go check on the uncles and make sure they know what they're doing."

"Don't mess up your tux," Ruby called after him.

As soon as the door slammed behind him, Ruby and Liam exchanged a tender smile.

"I wanted to tell you something before we renew our vows."

He studied her face. "I can tell there's something lying on your heart."

She reached out and entwined his hands with hers. "I've decided not to get recertified in search and rescue." She let out a deep breath. "That's all over for me now."

Liam's mouth opened. He fumbled for words. "What? But it's always been so important to you."

"It has been. And it was a wonderful career. But it was part of the past. My life is leading me in another direction."

"Are you sure about this? I want to make certain that you're fulfilled, not just in our home life but professionally, as well. That's important to me."

"I'll always value the work I did, but I don't want to take risks like that anymore. I want to close that chapter of my life. All I'll ever need to be fulfilled is you…

and Aidan and our faith. And whatever other little ones we may be blessed with down the road."

"Oh, Ruby, as long as it's something you're willingly letting go of… I'll never stand in your way. Not ever again."

"I know," she said with a fierce nod of her head. "You showed me that you would support all of my dreams and aspirations. It actually made my decision all the more meaningful, knowing that it was my decision to make."

She took a deep breath. "So that brings me to my next venture."

He raised an eyebrow. "Which is?"

"Training search-and-rescue dogs," she said in a triumphant voice. "Like Rufus."

Liam shook his head. He wasn't even surprised at his wife's ingenuity. Once a road closed she was planning to travel down another avenue. "That's a wonderful idea, Ruby. It's a nice way of staying tied to the search-and-rescue community. And with your love of dogs, it's perfect for you."

"I'm really excited about this, wherever it leads me. I've done a bit of dog handling before, but I'm really intrigued by all the possibilities." She crossed her hands in front of her. "I'm going to start small at first but, hopefully, I'll be able to really expand it into something much bigger. Hazel has been a real inspiration for me with her Lovely Boots."

Liam closed the gap between them and placed his hands on either side of Ruby's face. "Have I ever told you how much I love your tenacity? And your vision? There's nothing you can't do, Mrs. Ruby Prescott."

The door opened with a bang. "Smooching again?" Aidan asked with a loud groan. "Everyone is out there sitting in the pews. They're waiting for the wedding to start." He scrunched up his face. "Jasper is walking back and forth and mumbling to himself. He told me to tell you to get a move on."

Liam rolled his eyes. Ruby giggled and raised her hand to her mouth.

Liam locked eyes with Aidan. "Are you ready to do this?"

"I was born ready," Aidan said with a cocky tilt of his head.

Ruby chuckled. "Uh-oh. You've been hanging around Declan way too much."

"In the famous words of the mayor of this town, 'let's go get hitched,'" Liam said, placing his hand on Aidan's shoulder.

"Amen," Ruby said. "I can't wait to be your bride all over again."

A few minutes later Ruby walked down the aisle of the church to the strains of the "Wedding March." Kyle was at her side, ready to give her away to the man she adored.

As she walked past pews filled with friends and family members, she couldn't help but feel incredibly blessed. Her fears had all been put to rest. In the end, love had been her healing balm. The love she felt for Liam and Aidan stamped out all the darkness. And the tremendous way they adored her in return made her feel as if she could do anything...be anything. God had placed her exactly where she needed to be. She would never take it for granted again. Love, Alaska, was home.

Never again would she focus on the memories she had lost. From this moment forward she and Liam would be stepping toward their brilliant future, secure in the knowledge that nothing could ever shake this union or derail them from their path. From this point forward they would be walking in faith as husband and wife.

* * * * *

If you enjoyed REUNITED AT CHRISTMAS,
don't miss the other books in the
ALASKAN GROOMS *series:*

AN ALASKAN WEDDING
ALASKAN REUNION
A MATCH MADE IN ALASKA

Dear Reader,

Thank you for joining me on this journey to Love, Alaska. I truly hope you enjoyed Liam and Ruby's love story. I really enjoyed writing this reunion romance with a twist.

I love Christmas. It truly is the most wonderful time of the year. Peppermint hot chocolate. Decking the halls. Placing the star on top of the Christmas tree. Spreading cheer and goodwill. And above all, celebrating the birth of Christ.

Liam and Ruby's love story was one I really wanted to tell. Marriages go through tough times, and with love and faith, coupled with God's guiding light, we can work through these obstacles. Love really can move mountains.

Ruby Prescott is a woman who is searching for truth and family connections. The ties that bind us to the ones we love is a powerful theme. Although Ruby questions whether she truly belongs in Love, what she finds in the small fishing village is true, enduring love and happiness.

Although Liam has a clear view of the past, he's not certain of his future. He's bogged down by the mistakes of the past and his fear of Ruby remembering that their marriage wasn't perfect. What he learns is that God doesn't expect perfection from us. All of us are flawed, imperfect beings, but saved by God's grace.

Both Liam and Ruby needed faith to get them through the difficult questions surrounding the future of their marriage. Ultimately, they discover that love is truly the best gift of all.

I am honored to write for the Love Inspired line. It's been a dream come true. Being able to work in my pajamas is the best perk of the job.

I love hearing from readers, however you choose to contact me. You can reach me by email at scalhoune@gmail.com, at my Author Belle Calhoune Facebook page or at my website, bellecalhoune.com. If you're on Twitter, reach out to me @BelleCalhoune.

Blessings,
Belle

SPECIAL EXCERPT FROM

A promise to watch out for his late army buddy's little brother might have this single rancher in over his head. But he's not the only one who wants to care for the boy...

Read on for a sneak preview of the fourth book in the ***LONE STAR COWBOY LEAGUE: BOYS RANCH*** *miniseries, THE COWBOY'S TEXAS FAMILY by Margaret Daley.*

As Nick settled behind the steering wheel and started his truck, he slanted a look at Darcy. "So what do you think about the boys ranch?"

"Corey is much better off here than with his dad. He's not happy right now, but then he wasn't happy at home."

"He's scared." That was why Bea had brought him to the barn first to see Nick. "He'll feel better after he meets some of the other boys his age."

"What if he doesn't?" Darcy asked.

"He's confused. He wants to be with his dad, and yet not if he's always being left alone. He doesn't know what to expect from day to day and certainly doesn't feel safe." Those same feelings used to plague Nick while he was growing up.

"I've dealt with kids like that."

"In a perfect world, Ned wouldn't drink and would love Corey unconditionally. But that isn't going to hap-

LIEXP1216

pen. Ned isn't going to change." He knew firsthand the mind-set of an alcoholic and remembered the times his dad promised to stop drinking and reform. He never did; in fact he got worse.

"How do you know that for sure?"

"I just do." He didn't share his past with anyone. It was a part of his life he wanted to wipe from his mind, but it was always there in the background. He never wanted to see a child grow up the way he had.

"Then I'll pray for the best for Corey," Darcy said.

"The best scenario would be the state taking Corey away from Ned and a good family adopting him. I wish I was in a position to do it." The second he said that last sentence he wanted to snatch it back. He had no business being anyone's father.

"Because you're single? That might not matter in certain cases."

"I'm not dad material." How could he explain that he was struggling to erase the debt that his father had accumulated? If he lost the ranch, he would lose his home and job. But, more important, what if he wasn't a good father to Corey? It was one thing to be there to help when needed, but it was very different to be totally responsible for raising a child.

LIEXP1216